IKE MARS:
Bloody Key

I0526147

AIRSHIP 27 PRODUCTIONS

Ike Mars: Bloody Key
© 2019 Fred Adams Jr.

Published by Airship 27 Productions
www.airship27.com
www.airship27hangar.com

Interior illustrations © 2019 James McFarland
Cover illustration © 2019 Rob Davis

Editor: Ron Fortier
Associate Editor: Jonathan Sweet
Marketing and Promotions Manager: Michael Vance
Production and design by Rob Davis

ISBN-13: 978-1-946183-60-6
ISBN-10: 1-946183-60-1

Printed in the United States of America

10 9 8 7 6 5 4 3 2 1

IKE MARS:
Bloody Key

by Fred Adams Jr.

I

Pittsburgh is dismal every day, but in the cold rain of November, it's enough to drive good men to suicide. I can take the rain, and I can take the cold, but there's just something about the combination that eats through my skin and makes my bones ache. Being in Pittsburgh cranks it all up an extra notch.

Sure, it washes all the steel mill smoke out of the air, and all the coke oven cinders and chimney soot, and all the other crap the smokestacks belch out day and night, but where does it all go? Down the back of my neck with the rain water.

My name's Ike Mars. I'm a private eye in the aforementioned city, have been since I got kicked off the force two years ago in 1936 as part of a grand sweep that cleared out everyone on the force who wasn't a friend or lackey to the new Police Commissioner, Cap Agronski. People think Chicago politics are bad, and I admit, they have the patent on a few tricks and scams, but Pittsburgh makes Chicago look like a nursery school.

Out of a job, my former partner from the Detective Squad, Mason Cutter and I traded public buzzers for private ones. He and I aren't partners anymore, we just share an office, but we aren't competitors, either. Believe me, we're both busy, and there's still enough work for ten more PIs than Pittsburgh has already. It's a living, but I'm gonna miss my Police pension if I live long enough to need it.

The trouble with Pittsburgh in 1938 is you can't pin down one trouble to blame things on. Guys I know in the FBI say that for corruption, Pittsburgh's worse than Chicago. At least in Chicago the politicians wink and pretend they're on the level. It doesn't help much that in Pennsylvania, a case doesn't come to indictment unless the county District Attorney files the charges. Whoever owns the D.A. calls the shots.

Furthermore, in Pittsburgh the police don't investigate the police, and if you want to keep your private license, you better not either. So, I mostly chase bail skips, runaway kids, and wayward husbands. I'm still wearing last year's suit, but I'm eating okay, so who complains?

I do have one edge, though. They say lightning never strikes in the same place twice. How about the same person? I've been struck two times. Joey the Fish, a math whiz who's an odds maker for the Southside bookies says the odds against it are 790 grand to one. That makes me a special case already, but there's more.

Something went cattywampus in my wiring after the second hit, and I discovered one day that I can change my face. If I concentrate hard enough, I can make myself look like anybody I want. I can't change the rest of me, but I'll settle for my mug.

You can imagine how it helps me on surveillance; never the same face twice walking by or sitting on a bench on the street. I can look like anybody I want to get past security guards, receptionists, or anyone who might otherwise try to stop me. As a bonus, any time I'm late with my rent, I can walk right past the landlord and he never knows the difference.

Like most of these stories, it all started with a woman. Her name was Gloria Swenson, one vowel and about forty pounds away from the famous film star. Last month, she sashayed into my office and told me she was being blackmailed. Seems as if her hubby's chauffeur was driving her to some hot pillow joint in McKeesport and joining her for more than dinner and drinks.

The anonymous blackmailer had info but no pictures, which automatically made me suspicious of the chauffeur—Fritz was his name. I figured maybe Fritz was using a second party to squeeze the rich broad for some cash. I did a little digging and found out that Fritz was really Freddie Barnes, a gigolo who specialized in rich dames. The blackmailer called Gloria while Freddie was in the room, so he had a partner, a male partner.

I was trying to get a line on who that might be, so there I was on a blustery Wednesday night, on the South Side, headed for a meeting between Bobby Gorio, a mid-ladder hood, and someone he thought was Teddy "Two-Tone" Jones, but was really yours truly wearing Teddy's face. Bobby would give me a reliable line on the shakedown artist, believing it was all in the family.

The rain that night was a problem beyond the usual annoyance because I used white shoe polish to turn my black wingtips into Teddy's trademark two-tone shoes, and the rain was starting to wash off my disguise. The gusting wind added insult to injury.

I was hustling down Carson Street about ten o'clock, in a hurry to get to Bebe's Bar before my cover ran down the gutter, when a bleeding man staggered out of an alley and ran into me. It was Billy Cramer, a local second-story man. He had holes in his chest and the rain made the blood run like watercolors down his shirt.

He grabbed my coat sleeve, looked at my face and said, "Teddy! Thank God it's you. They shot me, but I got away." He pressed something into my hand. "Take this. Find it."

"Huh?"

"They're coming," he gasped. "Run." Billy let go of my coat and fell to the sidewalk.

I heard footsteps clattering in the alley, and I took Billy's advice and beat it. The people who shot him would drill me too if they thought I was helping him.

A gun went off, and a bullet zipped past my ear. Again, instinct took over. I pulled my piece and turned to shoot back. I snapped off a shot and the bad guys ducked behind a parked car. At that moment, the wind caught my hat and it sailed into the street.

I could hear sirens down the block. The gun thugs took off, but not before they got a good look at me. I was glad to be wearing someone else's face. I went back to Billy Cramer lying on the sidewalk, and when I felt for a pulse, there wasn't any. Too bad; I wanted to ask him what he meant by what were probably his last words.

I set my jaw and concentrated hard. I could feel things rearranging themselves, a feeling like snakes crawling under my skin, and in a few seconds, I was my old handsome self again. Just in time, too, because the prowl car pulled up to the curb and two cops in those goofy yellow rain slickers with the hoods that make them look like grade-school kids jumped out, pistols in hand. It occurred to me that they showed up just a little too fast. Maybe they just happened to be tooling down Carson on patrol, but I've learned to not believe in coincidences.

I laid my .38 on the sidewalk and stood, hands in the air. Too many of Pittsburgh's finest would love to have an excuse to put a hole through me, and do so with Cap Agronski's blessing.

'Well, well, well." One of the bulls shined a flashlight in my face. "If it ain't Dick Tracy, with an emphasis on 'Dick.'" It was John Kobylarz, Kobie to people who wanted to piss him off, one of Agronski's attack dogs.

"Now that you know it's me," I said, "mind if I get my hat?"

"You mean this one?" Jake Watts, Kobylarz's partner came around the back of the patrol car holding my fedora. Maybe we oughta take it in as evidence. Maybe the tire track on it matches the killer's car."

"Maybe it matches your prowl car. And who said anybody was killed, Watts? You seem to know a lot about it, or are you psychic all of a sudden?"

Kobylarz picked up my pistol. "I say somebody was killed, and I say you did it, smart guy."

"If that's true, then how did I run over my own hat, since I'm standing here."

A half dozen people had gathered in spite of the rain to gawk. Watts snarled, "Back off. Way back." The crowd complied.

At that moment, a dark Ford sedan pulled in behind the cop car. Two men in raincoats got out, holding their hats onto their heads in the wind. I was glad to see George Czap, homicide detective, and his partner Mike Montrose, two of my old colleagues who survived the Purge of '36. "Put your guns down," Czap said. They did, but they didn't really want to. I put my hands down.

"All right, Mars, what happened here?"

"We were driving down the block and heard shots. So, we hit the spinner and the siren and pulled right over. We found—"

"Shut up, Watts. I'm asking Mars." Watts looked like he'd been slapped.

"I was walking down the sidewalk when this guy stumbles out of that alley and falls on the sidewalk." I pointed to Billy. "Two guys with guns ran out after him and took a shot at me. I shot back."

"Bullshit," Kobylarz growled. "We pulled up, and Mars here was leaning over the dead guy."

"One more time, Kobie, who said he's dead? And why do you think I killed him?"

Montrose rolled Billy over. "He's dead, all right."

"And I'll bet you five bucks this is the murder weapon." Kobylarz held it up like a trophy."

Czap gave the body a cursory once over then turned to Kobylarz. "Let me see the gun."

He took a handkerchief from his pocket to wrap around the handle. Maybe I oughta take you in as a suspect, Kobie. I'll bet five bucks your prints are all over this weapon. Idiot." Czap flipped open the cylinder. "How many shots did you say you heard, Watts?"

"Uh, I didn't say."

"But you did say 'shots,' more than one."

"Uh, yeah."

Czap turned the gun so that the uniforms could see the cylinder. "One shot fired. I count three holes in the dead man." He snapped the .38 shut and turned to me. "You got another piece on you, Mars?"

"Nope." I made a show of opening my coat."Search me if you want.

"Not necessary." Czap turned to Watts. "Give him his hat."

Watts frowned and threw it to me. I caught it, punched it back into shape, and put it back on my head. The inside band was wet and cold.

"You know who that is on the sidewalk?" Czap asked the flatfeet. Both shook their heads. "You?" he asked me.

"Didn't get that far," I lied. "He looks familiar."

"He ought to," said Montrose, still kneeling by the body. "It's Billy Cramer."

"The burglar?" I feigned surprise.

"That's him." Montrose stood up. "I'll call the wagon." He headed for the unmarked car.

Czap shook his head. "Billy Cramer." He turned to the bystanders. "Any of you see anything?" No solid citizen stepped forward. No surprise. He eyed me for a second or two then said, "Come down to the station tomorrow, Mars. We'll need a statement." Czap handed me the pistol butt first.

"Wait a minute," said Kobylarz. "You're letting him walk?"

"Hell yes, I'm letting him walk. He's a licensed private investigator. Even he weren't, it's obvious to me, even if it isn't to you two stooges that he couldn't have shot the man three times with the same bullet."

As I walked away, Czap called after me, "Hey, Mars, don't leave town."

I shrugged. "Leave Pittsburgh? You're kidding me, right?" I laughed. "No place I'd rather be."

My meeting with Bobby Gorio was blown for that night. I pushed my hands into the pockets of my raincoat, and as I walked away, I ran my finger over the ridged edges of what Billy Cramer had given me: a bloody brass key.

Take this. Find it. First order of business: find out exactly what "it" is.

My '34 Plymouth coupe was waiting like a faithful old steed around the corner on 10th Street. The water sluicing over the bricks overran the gutters and sloshed over my feet—there went the last of the white polish—but I walked all the way around the car to make sure nobody was hiding behind the seat or on the running boards. I didn't bother looking under the car. Anybody hiding there was probably drowned by now.

I unlocked the suicide door and climbed inside, glad to be out of the rain. I started the engine and winced at the rumble of the bad muffler. The wiper made the view through the windshield worse instead of better.

Back in 1934 when I was still a detective and pulling down a good salary, I cleaned out my savings and bought the Plymouth for six hundred bucks. My first (and probably last) new car, unless some rich uncle I never met leaves me a bundle—or his new Cadillac. I sprung for the extra cash for the rumble seat, though nobody's ever sat in it, and a buck for a radio antenna.

Pittsburgh winters have taken their toll on the Clipper Blue paint; I never spent much time washing and waxing it anyway, and there's rust around a pair of bullet holes I never bothered to get patched. I figure it gives the car character. But the best feature of my Plymouth is the Philco radio I had installed in the dash that picks up all the commercial stations plus a police and fire band that comes in handy once in a while.

I turned on the radio and let it warm up along with the engine. I turned the dial and settled on 980, KDKA. They were running a live CBS broadcast of the Benny Goodman Quartet playing in the Roseland Ballroom in New York City. The King of Swing was blowing a sweet version of "Moonglow" on his clarinet while Lionel Hampton played cascading background riffs. I lit a Camel and waited 'til the song ended before I pulled away from the curb and headed for the 10th Street Bridge.

Driving across the bridge, I thought again, as I often did, that the round portals of the Armstrong Tunnels looked like the barrels of a shotgun aimed at my grille. The music cut out in the tunnel and bounced back again when I came out on the other side below the Bluff. The Quartet was barreling through "Sing, Sing, Sing," including a hot drum solo by Gene Krupa and the song lasted until I got to the Liberty Avenue garage where I keep my car.

Barney, the night attendant was dozing in his booth when I pulled in. I tapped the horn gently when I pulled up, and he popped up in the window like a prairie dog, a startled look on his face. "Oh, hello, Mister Mars." He straightened his cap, whose brim had fallen over the grey eyebrows that grew toward each other.

"Put her away for the night, Barney." I left the engine idling and stepped off the running board.

"Yes, sir." Barney shuffled around the front of the car, pushing his rimless spectacles up the bridge of his nose. He clambered into the driver's seat and let off the hand brake. With a ratcheting of gears, the coupe lurched forward into the depths of the garage. I just shook my head.

I keep my car in the Liberty Avenue garage because it's approximately the same distance from my apartment as it is from my office. I'd reached the point by that time of night where neither one was a particularly appealing destination. I turned my collar up against the cold rain and headed for Malone's.

I used to drink at the Shamrock, Pittsburgh's unofficial cop bar on Market Square, but an ex-cop in a cop bar is about as welcome as a wet dog in a wedding. Maybe it's because I'm a reminder that on any given day, any one of them could be out on the street from a shift in the political winds, a cut in the City's budget, or just pissing off any one of a thousand of the wrong people. Or maybe it's because I remind them that I'm not kissing ass anymore, and they are.

Malone's is what I would call an egalitarian bar. I like that word: egalitarian. My on-again off-again girl friend Marge Conway works for the *Pittsburgh Press* as a proofreader, and she knows more words than I'll ever read in my lifetime. She's always teaching me new words. She told me egalitarian means everybody getting treated the same. Anyway, that's the kind of bar Malone's is, egalitarian. Eddie Malone, the owner and bartender, abuses everyone equally. His insults have been known to make grown men whimper and bishops curse.

There are bars where people sit in a quiet funk and stare at their glasses more than they drink from them. At Malone's, if you sit still too long, Eddie will yell, "Hey, Jack, drink up or I'll charge you rent. You wanna play statue, go to the Greyhound station. They got lots of chairs."

I opened the door, and I stood on the threshold a second too long shaking off the rain.

"Shut the goddamn door. Heat costs money."

The radio behind the bar was blaring a blow by blow account of some prize fight, and a gang of the barflies were hooting and cheering as if they were watching it ringside.

I shucked off my coat and took a stool away from the radio crowd. Eddie came down the bar, and leaned in my face. He was five-six and built like a fireplug. His bald head shone in the neon lights over the bar like an electric tomato.

"Man from Mars," he cracked.

"Hey, Eddie. How's it going?"

"You wanna drink, Mars, or are you just here for the sparkling conversation?"

I laughed and said, "Boilermaker, Eddie. Bloop and a blast." I put a five-dollar bill on the bar.

Eddie went to the tap and pulled the Duke Beer handle. He never poured against the side of a glass; Eddie said it was a crime against nature to serve a beer without a head on it. He put the mug on the bar and went back for a shot glass and a bottle of my favorite whiskey, Seagram's Seven.

"I don't know why you drink that Canadian goose piss when there's good American whiskey all over the place."

"An acquired taste, Eddie." I started drinking Seagram's during Prohibition, when boatloads of it came sailing across Lake Erie like the Niña, Pinta, and the Santa Maria. Twelve hours by truck, and it was behind the bar at every Pittsburgh speakeasy. The Volstead Act was repealed, and the American breweries went back into production, but I never got out of the Seagram's habit.

"Here's to you." I raised my shot in a salute to Eddie and dropped the glass into the beer. It disappeared through the foam, and Eddie rolled his eyes.

"You like making work for me, don't you, Mars? How about next time I just pour the shot straight into the beer and only have to wash one glass, not two?"

"Naah, I like yanking your chain 'cause you're so cute when you're pissed off."

"Christ." Eddie moved down the bar to harangue some of the fight fans into buying another round.

I pulled the key out of my pocket and studied it in the dim light of the bar. The head of the key was a perfect rectangle, an inch wide and three-quarters tall. The shaft was maybe an inch and a quarter. The key wasn't ground from a blank, it was hand crafted by a pro. The back side of the key was stained with a smear of dried blood. If somebody was willing to kill Billy Cramer for it, it was worth investigating.

One drink down, and Eddie brought another.

I felt a blast of clammy air, and I heard Eddie shout, "Shut the goddamn door." In the mirror over the bar, I saw Kobylarz and Watts shouldering through the doorway. Call it instinct, call it inspiration, call it Divine guidance; I dropped the key into my mug and watched it disappear through the foam.

The flatfeet came up behind me, one on each side. "Hands on the bar, Mars," Watts growled in my ear. "No funny moves."

"I thought you guys'd be at the Shamrock by now."

The barflies suddenly got quiet. The radio blared on.

Kobylarz reached into my coat and pulled my .38 out of the holster.

"I want a receipt."

Watts cuffed me on the back of my head with the heel of his hand. "You don't need one. This time, you won't get it back, smart guy."

Each one took an elbow and hauled me off the bar stool. Eddie hurried over. "What the hell's going on?"

Kobylarz shot back, "Police business, bud. Mind your own."

As they hauled me out the door, I called over my shoulder, "Save my drink for me, Eddie. I'll be back for it."

They took me down the sidewalk and around the corner to an unlighted doorway and shoved me through. The door closed behind us, and I found myself in a grocery store back room full of crates and boxes of produce. Bins of onions and potatoes stood against one wall, and a bunch of bananas hung from a chain in the ceiling.

Watts stood in front of me, chin to chin. "Okay, Mars. Where is it?" Kobylarz circled behind me.

"Hell if I know. I don't even know what 'it' is. Give me a hint."

"I'll give you a hint." Kobylarz whacked me across the backs of my knees with a nightstick, and I went into Communion position. Kobylarz grabbed the lapels of my jacket and pulled it halfway down my arms, pinning them against my sides. Watts punched me in the jaw and almost tipped me over.

"Don't knock him out, dummy, at least not yet." Kobylarz grabbed a handful of my hair and bent my head back to look at him upside down. "You took something from Willy Cramer's body, and we want it."

"I didn't take anything from Willy Cramer or anybody." Which was true; he gave it to me, and technically, I didn't take it.

"You're lying," Watts hissed. "Stand him up."

Kobylarz yanked me to my feet and Watts said "One more time, Mars. Tell us where it is."

"One more time, Watts, I don't know what 'it' is."

Kobylarz rammed the end of his Billy club into my gut and I doubled over, glad I hadn't had time to finish the second beer, or it would have been all over my shoes. "Pull out his pockets."

Watts turned my trouser pockets inside out, and change jingled on the concrete and rolled in every direction. My pocket watch dangled from its chain. My right back pocket is sewn three quarters shut in all of my trousers to make a holster for my sap. Watts threw it over his shoulder and it landed with a dull thunk on the floor.

I was glad I dumped the key into the beer. They'd have to keep me alive at least 'til they found it. If I had it on me now, I'd be dead in five minutes or less.

He rifled my coat pockets and pulled my wallet out of one side and the fold over with my badge and license from the other. He pulled money, business cards, receipts, and a dozen other pieces of paper from the wallet and let them all flutter to the floor.

"Take off your pants," Kobylarz snarled.

"Okay," I wheezed, my diaphragm still twitching from the nightstick. "Gotta take off my coat. Suspenders."

"Go ahead."

I slipped my left arm out of the sleeve. "You guys made a mistake, Kobie."

"You hear that, Watts? We made a mistake. What mistake was that?"

"You didn't cuff me."

At the word "cuff," I threw my suit coat over Kobie's head and in the same comprehensive motion, turned and kicked Watts' balls somewhere close to his liver. Kobylarz was out from under the coat, but not fast enough to tag me with the nightstick. It swished past my head as I stepped in and caught him under his eye with a right hook. He staggered backward and tripped on a crate of lettuce.

Watts was lying on his side, both hands clutching his crotch. He let go with one hand and reached for his service revolver. I kicked him again, this time under his chin. I heard his teeth clip together. His eyes rolled back in his head and he was out of the action.

I wasn't so lucky with Kobylarz. He had his pistol halfway out of the holster. I dodged to the side and grabbed the bananas, swinging them in front of me as he fired. The fruit stopped the bullet, and I did a duck and roll as he fired again, the shot ricocheting off the floor.

I crouched behind a three-high pile of crates with CABBAGE stenciled on the side.

"Come on out, Mars. You got no place to go."

Keep him talking. "Or what? You'll shoot me? You can't do that, Kobie. You need me alive."

"Maybe I'll just shoot you in the foot, or maybe both of 'em. Come out and make it easy on yourself."

Come on, Kobie, I thought, just one step closer. I leaned against the crates, a hand on the top and middle ones. "You won't hurt me if I give up?"

"That's right. Come out and I won't hurt you."

Bingo. Right where I wanted him. I tipped the crates forward, and they fell on Kobylarz, knocking him on his back. I dove over the crates and grabbed his wrist. He and I fought for the gun, but because his left arm was pinned under a hundred pounds of cabbage and two hundred pounds of me, the fight didn't last long. I wrestled the pistol free with both hands and clubbed him in the forehead with it.

I pushed the muzzle up his nostril. "Your turn, Kobie. Tell me about 'it.'"

"I—I"

I cocked the hammer. "One, two . . ."

"It's a key. A key." Kobylarz was whining now.

"Wrong 'it.' A key to what?"

"I don't know. I swear I don't. On my mother's grave."

"I'll bet she's rolling over in it. Who's in charge?"

"I don't know. We never saw the guy. Only talked to him. He called me at a pay phone. We met him down under the Bridge last night."

"What bridge?"

"Liberty. Liberty Bridge. He was in the back of a car."

"What kind of car? Make? Model? Color?"

"I don't know, it was dark."

"You were supposed to kill Billy Cramer?"

"No, nobody was supposed to kill anybody. We were just supposed to brace him and get the key. I swear it's true."

"And the other guys who shot at me?"

"I don't know," he wailed, tears leaking from his eyes and running into his ears. "It was just supposed to be me and Watts."

I believed him for no other reason than he was right about the key and he was too dumb to make up the rest. "Find another job, Kobie. You stink at this one."

I hit him a little harder with the pistol this time, and he quit whining.

I picked up my money, my papers, and my sap and put them all back where they belonged. I found my .38 in Watts' trouser pocket, and it went back into the holster. As an afterthought, I cuffed the two unconscious flatfeet together and stuffed bananas from the bunch in the breast pocket of both their uniform tunics. I took their shields as proof of my story. Czap was going to be very interested in those two tomorrow.

Nobody on the street. The cold rain was still pounding like buckshot. I turned the corner and went back inside Malone's. The fight on the radio was over, and the crowd had thinned out. A half dozen die-hards still slumped at the bar.

I put my arms through the sleeves of my coat and jammed my hat on my head.

"Glad you came back, Mars," Eddie said. "You forgot your change. Next thing I know, you'll accuse me of stealing it from you."

He held out his palm with a two-dollar bill and some coins in it. Eddie winked, and only I saw it. Under the bill was the key.

I left Malone's and headed for 5th Avenue. I knew better than to go home or to my office at the moment. I'd had enough surprises for one night. I figured my best bet for a safe haven was The Mingott. The Mingott hotel was an inch above flop house status, but it was an unlikely place for people to look for me. I'd put clients up there once or twice when they didn't want to be found by process servers or angry wives, and Ronnie, the night manager, knew me.

I laughed at the sign in the lobby window: These fifty-cent-a-night rooms must be seen to be appreciated. I pushed into the revolving door and it spun me into the lobby. The Mingott was a respectable place for traveling businessmen back in the boom times of the 90s, but the Depression had hit it just as hard as anyplace else, and its decline accelerated. The velvet drapes were dusty and the marble floor was cracked, but as one light bulb after another flickered out in the crystal chandelier and went unreplaced, the joint looked better every time I came through the door.

Ronnie sat behind the desk, his yellowed buck teeth forming a perpetual muskrat grin. Stray threads of his moth-eaten suit stuck out like wires in a punctured window screen. The little scarecrow was guarding the board with thirty or so keys on hooks. Guy Lombardo oozed from the big Zenith radio across the lobby. Ronnie looked up as I came in. "Mars." He made an elaborate show of looking around me to one side then the other. "Got a client in the car?"

"No, Ronnie, just me. I need a room for the night."

"Times must be really tough if you're staying here. And the President said on the radio just this afternoon that things are starting to turn around. Damn."

"Got one with a view?"

"Sorry, just leased out the Presidential Suite an hour ago. How about 217?" He reached for the key.

"Sure." I dropped a fifty-cent piece on the counter. "The elevator work?" It was a regular joke.

"Not since '37." he chuckled. "I'd ring for the bellboy, but you don't have any bags."

"You'd have to hire one first. I'll take the stairs. That's easier than the fire escape."

I figured my best bet for a safe haven was The Mingott.

Ronnie called after me. "Do you want a wake-up call?"

"No, Ronnie. I'll just let nature take its course."

Room 217 was, like all the Mingott's rooms, small, so the door opened outward into the hallway. That suited me. I locked it and leaned the room's one straight-backed chair against it so that if anybody opened the door, the chair would fall and wake me, and the uninvited guest would be blocked and distracted long enough for me to shoot him.

I took off my jacket and flopped on the bed, shoes and all. Speaking of uninvited guests, I wished I had rubber bands to pull over my cuffs to keep the cockroaches from climbing up my trouser legs. I fell asleep with my hand on my revolver and didn't move the rest of the night.

I woke with a headache that was second only to the sore jaw where Watts socked me the night before. I raised the window blind and saw that the rain had stopped, but the sky was a uniform shade of grey. I decided I needed a shower and a change of clothes and some breakfast before I went to the station to meet with Czap and Montrose. I pulled on my coat and took the stairs to the Mingott's lobby.

The day clerk, a stooped old codger named Raymond was huddled over a copy of the *Press* reading it through a big brass magnifying glass. I dropped the key on the desk. "217." I said. He looked at me, then the key, then back at me again, as if he were doing me a favor by accepting it.

I shrugged and walked through the revolving door and it pushed me out onto the sidewalk and into the bleak morning.

In ten minutes, I was at my building. I didn't go in, though because I saw a cop car parked out front. It may have absolutely nothing to do with me, I thought, but I ducked into the alley and changed my face to look like one of my neighbors. No sense taking chances, in case Watts and Kobylarz were stupid enough to file charges on me. The two uniforms standing by the car eyed me up, but they didn't say anything as I passed them and went into the building. The elevator stopped at my floor, and when the doors opened, I saw two more cops standing outside my apartment. I let the doors close and pushed the button for the lobby. So much for a shower and a change of clothes.

I kept my neighbor's face as I walked to the garage. A squad car was sitting out front. Okay, I thought. Maybe I should call Czap and ask him what's going on. I found an empty phone booth and dropped a nickel in the slot. I asked for Czap, and the desk sergeant put him on the line.

"Yeah."

"George?"

There was a long pause. "Mars, is that you?"

"Yeah, it's me. Wanna tell me what the hell's going on? There are cops at my apartment and my garage. I'd bet they're sitting outside my office too."

"And you'd be right, Ike. There's a warrant out on you for murder."

A chill ran through me, and it wasn't the weather. "Murder? Who?"

"Your playmates from last night, Kobylarz and Watts. Want to tell me about it?"

"Wait a minute, George. I didn't kill anybody."

"Turn yourself in, Ike. I'll do what I can to keep the bulls downstairs from pulling off your arms."

"Okay, don't believe me." I know how cops think. I used to be one. I was the easy collar. People at Malone's saw the Bobbsey Twins drag me out of the place. "Yeah, we fought, but when I left, they were both breathing."

"So you say."

"Have they autopsied Kobylarz and Watts? What caliber gun was used to kill them?"

Czap paused again. I could hear the scratch of a pencil on paper. "No autopsy yet. Maybe this afternoon. But Kobie's gun had two rounds fired. He and Watts got one each."

"I'm telling you, George, I didn't do it."

"Listen, Ike. Maybe you're telling me the truth, maybe you aren't. I can't help you if you're on the street. Nobody can, and you'll be a target for every cop in the City."

"If I turn myself in, I'll be dead in a day. Whoever's behind this will have me iced to cover his tracks. Case closed, and he skates. Do you want that?"

George was quiet for a long time before he finally said, "Ike, I could probably be fired just for talking to you. You change your mind, call me. I'll meet you somewhere and bring you in myself, and do everything I can to see you get a fair shake."

"In our egalitarian court system? Don't make me laugh." I hung up the phone.

I could almost hear the sound of knives on a whetstone in the office of Ambrose Jeffers, the most crooked D.A. since courts were invented. Jeffers would try this one himself; a bad apple P.I., a cop killer. He'd ride it all the way to the Governor's mansion.

George was honest, at least as honest as a Pittsburgh cop could be, but because he was honest, his juice was limited. Protect me? Not likely if that conflicted with someone else's best interest. The Boys in Blue would open my cell door, drag me out, and shoot me in a bogus jailbreak. Or put some hitter in my cell to shank me in my sleep and say it was self-defense. No way was I going to turn myself in.

He was right about one thing, though, every cop in the 'Burgh would be looking for Ike Mars. I just had to stay somebody else.

That could be a tall order all by itself. I learned in the last year that I could change my face, but there were limits. More than an hour or two, and it starts to hurt; much longer, and it hurts like hell. No free lunches. And it starts to slip. Also, if I hold a face too long, I have to wait a while before I can put on another one. I could keep my neighbor's mug for a while yet, but I'd have to find someplace safe to turn back into good old Ike for a while.

I picked up a copy of the *Post Gazette* at the newsstand where I usually buy my papers. Johnny, the little weasel who runs the stand also runs numbers for Lou Mercante. He took my money looking me right in the face and didn't blink.

I stepped into Morrie's Coffee Shop and slid into a booth. Sally the waitress, somebody else who saw my face just about every day, sidled up with her order pad. "What'll you have, Mac?"

She didn't recognize me either, or she would have brought a cup of coffee right off and followed it with a plate of scrambled eggs and bacon with hash browns on the side, like she has four days out of five for the past ten years.

"Uh, pancakes and coffee."

She jotted the order down. "Coming up."

I unfolded the paper. The big headlines were City Attorney Rosenwasser getting kickbacks—no surprises there, and Republicans promising an investigation into the link between relief and politics. No mention of two dead cops. Too soon for the morning papers, I thought, but it would be across the top of the *Press* and the *Sun-Telegraph* afternoon editions.

Sally brought my breakfast. I didn't feel much like eating, but once I started, I shoveled the food in like coal into a boiler. I guess I was hungrier than I thought, and still being alive made even the plainest food a banquet. After a second cup of coffee, I paid the check and went to the back of the restaurant and the pay phone next to the men's room door.

I dialed the number for the *Pittsburgh Press*. "Marge Conway, please." I figured Marge would be able to tell me what the newspapers were saying before I could read it myself.

The line clicked. "This is Marge Conway."

"Hi, Margie." I used my pet name for her—which she hated and didn't allow anyone to use but yours truly—so she'd know it was me without mentioning my name.

"My God," she gasped. "Where are you? Are you all right?"

"Close by and fine."

"I was proofing this afternoon's edition. The cops have an all-out manhunt going for you."

"Marge, I didn't—"

"Don't tell me." she snapped. "Because I'll believe you, and that'll make it that much harder watching you die and knowing you're innocent."

"Okay." I gave it a three-count. "Can you just tell me what the article says?"

"I can do better than that. I'll read it to you. The proof's still in the tray." Marge set the phone down, and I heard some paper shuffling. She came back on the line.

"Headline: Two Cops Dead in Execution Murder. Second head: Private Eye Sought in Slaying."

"Here's the story: Police are searching the city for a private investigator they say is wanted for the murder of two unidentified Pittsburgh City Police Officers. The men were shot to death execution-style in the rear of McMonigle's Grocery Store on Maybry Street. The unidentified officers were found handcuffed together on the floor of the grocery's storeroom, both dead from single gunshots to the head. The pair appeared to have been beaten severely before they were killed."

"They got that part right."

"Shut up and listen." She went on, "'The suspect, private investigator Ike Mars of Pittsburgh is at still at large and has become the subject of the most intense manhunt in the City's history. Police Commissioner William 'Cap' Agronski has vowed, 'The Department will pull out all the stops to find this [expletive deleted] and put him in the electric chair.'"

I could just imagine Agronski standing in front of the station with all his brass buttons shined up for the cameras and Jeffers right beside him. "'Autopsies today are expected to confirm that the officers were shot with a police service revolver. The identities of the dead policemen are being withheld until—'"

I broke in. "I'll give you a scoop. Want their names? Kobylarz and Watts."

"God, no. I don't want anything but to see you get out of this mess alive." Her voice caught on the last word, and I wanted to reach through the phone and take her face in my hands. "The *Press is* running a picture of you, Ike, from when you were still on the force. The whole city's going to be hunting for you, cops and civilians alike."

"Take my word for it, Marge. Nobody's gonna see my face in this town."

Marge was one of the few people who knew about my special ability, and she got the drift of my comment. "Okay. What can I do to help you?"

"Right now, just act normal."

"Oh sure." I could see her eyes rolling right through the receiver."

"Go about your job and everyday routine. The cops'll come by, maybe watch your apartment, maybe follow you to see if you'll lead me to them. Look, I'll have a better handle on all this in a few hours. There's a phone booth at 12th Street and Penn. Here's the number. I rattled it off. I'll call you at four. They'll tap your phone, and my phone at the apartment and the office. Normally, it'd take a while to get a court order for a wiretap, but I have a feeling that somebody's pulling big strings on this case."

"Be careful, Ike." I could hear the tears in her voice.

"Always, Marge." I hung up the phone before I teared up too.

There I was with thirty bucks in my wallet, five bullets in my gun, a key to I don't know what plus two dead cops' badges in my pocket, and somebody else's face on my skull. Business as usual.

IV

The Turkish baths on Liberty Avenue are a good place to do business if you're worried about weapons as a tool of negotiation. It's tough to hide a knife or a gun under those skimpy towels they give you. I've never had a conference there myself, but I do find it a good place to rent a locker under the same of Bill Smith. In it I keep a change of clothes, two pistols, a .32 and a .38, and a two hundred-dollar bills sewn into the cuff of a waist-length jacket.

The baths are up a narrow flight of stairs on the second floor over the Dobbs Hat Shop. Inside, the walls are white tile, and the floors are done up in those little black and white hexagons that make a weird kind of checkerboard. The air is about thirty degrees warmer than the outside, and it smells of hot iron pipes, sweat, and eucalyptus oil.

The locker room is off to the side. It was early in the day and the place wasn't too busy. I went in and found two men, a big, hairy guy drying himself and the other undressing on the bench that ran the length of the narrow room. Neither was near my locker, so I sat down and started unlacing my shoes.

"Did you hear the radio today, Bob?" the big guy asked, pulling a towel side to side across his ass as if he were polishing it. Out front, his manhood swung side to side as he did, proving Newton's theory that for every action, there is an equal and opposite reaction.

"Yeah," the other guy said. "That was something about that private eye killing those two cops. I hope they catch the bastard and fry him."

I knew for a fact that one would logically follow the other, since the Commonwealth of Pennsylvania had the highest execution rate in the country, averaging one hundred sixty-seven a year this decade. I would have to pull out every trick in the bag to keep from getting caught if I was going to avoid a ride in the hot seat.

I decided I didn't want to just open the locker, change my clothes and leave. That might look suspicious to these two, and besides, I thought an hour in the steam room might do me some good, give me some space to think. I opened the locker and hung my coat on one of the hooks. I patted the jacket hanging inside and felt the pistol in an inside pocket. I turned my back to Bob and his buddy and slipped my shoulder rig off with my suit jacket.

My pants came next, then my drawers. I took a fresh towel from the shelf inside the door, and as an afterthought, took a second one.

Bob from the locker room was alone in the steam room when I got there. I nodded to him and took a seat on the top tier. The room was tiled, floor, ceiling and walls, and half was occupied by a kind of stair step arrangement to allow seating in tiers, like bleachers in a stadium. I put a towel across my lap. Then I leaned my head back against the tile and draped the second towel over my face.

It felt good, changing back. I could feel the muscles in my face relaxing and the dull ache subside. I'd just have to wait 'til my companion left before I took away the towel so he wouldn't see the real me.

The key. It was the answer to the whole riddle. If I could find out what lock it fit, I'd know why Billy was killed, why Kobylarz and Watts were killed, and why I was still in danger of getting killed. I knew two first-rate locksmiths. Fats Marshall was pretty chummy with the cops; he did most of the P.D. work, but Jack Lasner worked both sides of the street, though try as they might, the cops could never catch him. We understood each other, and he was somebody I could trust to not blow the whistle on me.

I was glad I didn't mention the key or what Kobylarz told me about Billy to Czap. Having the key gave me a reason to kill the flatfeet. Having the key fingered me for killing Cramer to get it. It was a two-bladed axe, and whichever way it swung, it would have chopped off my head.

Half an hour in the heat and Bob left me alone in the swirling white clouds. I figured I'd give him fifteen minutes; he should be dressed and out by then. I concentrated on my neighbor's face and felt mine twisting into shape. I pulled away the towel, and climbed down from my perch.

I was nearly dressed when a voice called out behind me. "Ray? Hey, I didn't know you came here."

I turned, and saw a chubby guy in a suit a half size too small for him with a top coat over his arm.

I nodded. "Just started today." Who the hell was this guy?

"Oh yeah?" He frowned. "You sound bad. Got a cold?"

I coughed. "Uh, bronchitis. Thought maybe the steam would help."

He opened a locker and hung his coat in it. "That's too bad. It's this weather. I had the sniffles myself a couple days ago. Tell Alice to make you a hot toddy. That'll be good for you."

I grunted. I still had to get my shoulder rig on and I was pretty sure Ray didn't carry a gun as a regular order of business. I fiddled around retying my shoelaces while he undressed.

"How do you like Father Broznic?"

"Uh okay."

"That was some homily he gave last Sunday. Pretty tough for a new priest, huh?"

"Unh." I had to get rid of this guy. I turned his direction and launched into a coughing fit that startled both of us, and he stepped back, afraid I might be contagious. He quickly slipped out of his skivvies, threw them into his locker, grabbed a towel and headed out the door.

"See you later, Ray. Remember what I said about the toddy."

V

In five minutes, I was back on the street. I caught a cab across town to Squirrel Hill and had the cabbie drop me off on Murray at a long block of storefronts. I put my face back during the ride, and the driver gave a me a funny look when I handed him the fare. "Keep the change."

"Thanks, Mac." As he pulled away from the curb, I could see him craning his neck to gawk at me in the mirror.

The one I was looking for had a sign over the sidewalk that said simply "Locksmith." In the narrow front window, I saw a big ring of heavy skeleton keys hanging beside a sign that said, "Jail Keys Made Here."

A spring bell dinged overhead when I walked in. Jack wasn't behind the counter that divided the store. "Lockie!" I called. "You back there?"

"Where else would I be? Keep yer pants on. I'll be out in a minute."

Behind the counter, Jack kept a floor-to-ceiling shadow box arrangement filled with an assortment of parts and hardware. Every compartment was labeled, and every item was neatly placed. Jack had come to Pittsburgh from Brooklyn years before, and swore every week that he was ready to pack up and go back, but he never did. "At least in Brooklyn, people smiled when they stuck a knife in you."

The curtain to the back room swung away and Jack came out, all ninety-eight pounds of him. Frail was one word you might apply to him if you didn't know better. Wiry was more accurate. Jack was little but New York tough, as more than one local found out the hard way. He had a magnifier on a strap around his head and the vest from what had once been an expensive suit over a T-shirt. The handles of a pair of needle nosed pliers poked out of one pocket.

"Okay, pal, what can I—" He froze. His eyes, usually just slits in his forehead opened wide. "Mars."

"You heard, huh?"

"Who hasn't? It's all over the radio. You knocked off two blue boys."

"I didn't do it."

"Did I ask? I don't give a damn whether you did or not. I didn't know the Pollack, but Watts was a shit heel. I figure his partner came from the same litter. Good riddance." There was no love lost between Jack and the police.

I laughed in spite of myself. "Well, if you heard that, you heard I'm number one on the Most Wanted List."

He nodded, "Uh huh. So, quick, before the cops come in here guns blazing and put a hole in me as an innocent bystander, whattaya need?"

"Two things. I need copies of a key, and I need your expert advice on what lock it opens."

"Lemme see it."

I handed Jack the key and he turned it over in his fingers. "It's not a safe-deposit key, if that's what you were hoping. It looks automotive, but this wasn't ground out of a pre-cast blank. It's been milled from sheet brass. Nice work, by the way." He looked up. "And no, I didn't make it." He ran his thumb over the angular ridges, then pulled his magnifier down over his left eye. He squinted through the lens, turning the key one way then the other. "The cuts are made by hand, used a jeweler's file. There's no shoulder stop. The tip of the key sets the depth."

"Can you copy it?"

"Hell, yeah I can. It'll take a while, though."

"You said it looks like a car key. Any idea on the make?"

He turned the key around and rubbed the rectangle between his thumb and forefinger. "If the bow was an octagon, it would be a Chevy ignition key. Square, a Ford. Scalloped, a Chrysler. Round, it could be a Studebaker, or a trunk key for a dozen models. A lot of cars have a different shape for the ignition and the trunk. Hard to tell what it is, offhand."

"I want you to make me two copies. But not exact."

Jack blinked. "Huh?"

"I want them to look good, but I don't want them to open the lock."

"So, you want two dummy keys that look just like this one." He juggled the key one-handed. "I can do that. I guess you need it yesterday, huh?"

"Yesterday would be good, but I'll settle for whatever you can manage for me."

"Come back in three hours. I might have the brass stock in the back, if not I'll have to go pick it up. I'll get on it right away."

"Thanks, Lockie."

"Gonna cost you, Mars."

"A bargain at the price."

"Good thing you didn't say 'cheap,' or I'd 'a charged you double for the insult."

I stepped out onto the sidewalk, and as I did, Lockie turned the sign on the door from Open to Closed.

The rain had started again, a chilly drizzle that dotted my jacket. The sidewalks were crowded in spite of the lousy weather. I turned my collar up and pulled my hat down low, hoping nobody recognized me.

I fished in my pocket for a nickel and ducked into a phone booth at the end of the block. I dialed my office number and let it ring a half dozen times, hoping Mason Cutter might pick it up. It was always kind of a game when we were both in the office; whoever got to the phone first when a prospective client called got the job.

"Hello." It was Mason. I didn't hear the telltale click of an extra phone or any drop in volume. No tap on the phone yet.

"Mister Mars, please."

"Not here, but I expect him any time now. Would you like to leave a number so he can call you back?"

I read the number off the pay phone dial, and I heard the scratch of a pen on paper. "And may I ask who's calling?"

"Honus Wagner."

"Yes, Mister Wagner. I'll have him call you as soon as he comes in." He hung up. Mason knew my voice as well as his own sweet mother's. He wasn't alone in the office. Cops. I could imagine him sitting at the desk with the earpiece pressed tight against his head to keep the flatfeet from hearing my end of the conversation. Mason was sharp enough to jot down a bogus number and keep the real one in his head.

Ex-cops are often the biggest headache for current ones. Cops go by the book, and if you know the drill as well as Mason and I do, a little imagination goes a long way to cut the legs from under an investigation.

If the cops were sitting in the office, I didn't expect Mason to call me back anytime soon, but I'd stop by on the hour, our regular procedure when either of us was out, and wait for the phone to ring.

In the meantime, I needed to find a dry place to hide out. I headed for Forbes and the Squirrel Hill branch of the Carnegie Library.

For anything bad that people might say about Andrew Carnegie, his funding of libraries, schools, and other resources to help anybody learn and improve himself shouted it down in my estimation. Do-gooders might argue with me, but I agree with Carnegie's theory that what he did was better than handouts any day. Feed somebody's gut for a week, or feed his head for the rest of his life and make a better place for himself. Egalitarian. The library was open to anyone, even a fugitive.

I was still wearing my own face, which was a luxury that would evaporate as soon as the afternoon papers hit the street. Marge said the *Press* was running a picture of me on the front page, and the *Sun-Telegraph* would surely run one too.

So, I had the cops after me, whatever mystery man had Kobylarz and Watts on the pad, and another set of hitters working for someone else. Too many doors to watch at once. Then it hit me. Teddy Two-tone was in danger from the hoods who shot at me and saw his face instead of mine. There was an angle I could work.

It took me three tries to find a phone booth that still had an intact directory hanging from a chain. The first, someone put a match to. The second was missing altogether. The third was in a booth in a drugstore where nobody could swipe it easily. I found the number for Bebe's, where I hoped to find Bobby Gorio. I dialed the number, and Sal, the bartender, picked up on the third ring.

"Bebe's." Noise in the background told me that the bar was busy already, but with three full shifts running at J&L, the place could have been busy twenty-four hours a day.

"Is Bobby Gorio there?"

"Who wants to know?"

"Somebody who's gonna come over there in ten minutes and kick your greasy Wop ass if you give me any more static, Sal. Go get him."

"All right, all right." I heard Sal put his hand over the mouthpiece and a muffled "Bobby," followed by something I couldn't hear, probably questioning my father's identity.

"This is Gorio. Who's this?"

"Never mind. You see Teddy Two-Tone, tell him there's a contract out on him."

"Who put it out?"

"Dunno, Bobby. Just warn him." I hung up the phone. That should start a few gears turning. I had two reasons for pulling that stunt. One, my feeling of responsibility for siccing the gunsels on Teddy and putting him at risk, and the other, the thought that if he shot back when they came after him, I might get lucky and he'd take part of the Trifecta off my tail.

The library was quiet, as you might expect. I took the new copy of *Time* off the magazine shelf and headed into the reading room. I found one empty armchair. The rest were occupied by bums dozing away the rainy afternoon. Not exactly what Carnegie had in mind.

I eyeballed the cover. A picture of Andre Malraux, the French politician. I leafed through the magazine, figuring I'd find something of interest to read. Generalissimo Francisco Franco's brother Ramon was killed in a plane crash, Adolph Hitler was looking to colonize overseas territory, and China and Japan were still beating each other bloody.

"Is Bobby Gorio there?"

I skipped past those articles; what caught my eye was a piece on the aftermath of the Mercury Radio Theater broadcast of *The War of the Worlds*, which set half the country in a panic a week earlier. I missed the broadcast myself, but I heard enough about it from other people. Orson Welles caused an enormous upset with a too realistic Halloween broadcast of a Martian invasion. Big deal. In a week everybody'll be up in arms over something else, and in six months, they'll forget it ever happened.

When it got near three o'clock, I held the magazine up in front of my face and for the sake of variety, focused on Andre Malraux and pasted his mug on me. One of the bums did a double take when I put the magazine down. Maybe he recognized the Frog.

I went into the phone booth on Murray and held the earpiece to my head as if I were talking to someone while I held the hook down with my finger. No ring. Try again at four. I decided to try Lasner to see whether he was done with the bogus keys.

The sign on the door was turned to open; a good omen. I walked past the shop and ducked into an alley to switch faces. When I went in the shop, he came through the curtain as soon as the bell rang. "I got your keys for you, Mars. You got a real piece of my art here." He slapped three keys on the counter. "Which one's the original?"

I stared at the three keys. I couldn't tell them apart.

"I antiqued the brass with vinegar and salt water so they'd match the first one. Look alike, don't they?"

"I can't tell them apart."

"Take a guess."

I pointed to the one in the middle. "That one."

"Lucky guess, Mars. It is this one." He picked it up in one hand and one of the copies in the other. He put them side to side. Look close at the second ridge. It's only a hair shorter than the original, but it won't quite reach the pin."

"You're sure?"

He looked at me out of the tops of his eyes. "Who you talking to here, Mars? By the way, the key's for a Hudson trunk, maybe a '34 or '35 Hornet or Terraplane."

"Really?"

"I have a bunch of old car locks in the back from wrecks and junkers I keep to replace them when people lose their keys,"

"Good work. What do I owe you?"

"You're a little short on bucks at the moment aren't you? Being on the run, I mean."

I nodded. "Yeah, but—"

"No buts about it." He put up his hands, palms forward. "I know you well enough to know you'll pay me if you get through this alive, and I know you well enough to know you will."

"Okay, Lockie. Thanks."

He made a shooing motion with his hands. "Now beat it before somebody sees me talking to you and locks me up as some kind of accessory."

So I didn't mix them up, I put the real key in one pocket and the fakes in the other. The rain was falling steadily now, and I turned up my collar and went back to the phone booth. I passed a corner vending machine and saw the headline on the *Sun-Telegraph*: Two Cops Slain, P.I. at Large. And there was my picture, a formal pose from my uniform days, short hair cut, blue tunic with a Sam Browne belt, and my peaked cap under one arm. Did I always look so sinister? Or did the *Sun-Telegraph* jigger the picture to make me look meaner? Good thing for me that early November brought early darkness.

I waited out the call in the booth. The phone rang at four on the dot. "Mason?"

"You really stuck your dick in the fan this round, Ike. The cops sat in the hall all day. I haven't been outside yet, but I'm betting there's a car full out front. George Czap and Montrose just left the office ten minutes ago. Czap gave me some song and dance about wanting to help you. I just played dumb, which, granted, doesn't take much effort."

"Where are you now?"

"Two doors down. The insurance agent left for the day. The door lock's just like ours. Only took me five seconds. Now, give me the lowdown."

For the next ten minutes, I filled him in on the whole deal. When I finished, he was quiet for a minute, then he let out a long gust of air. "Like I said about the fan."

I looked at my watch. "Oh, hell, I forgot I have to call Marge. Call me back in five minutes."

"You think she'll be done reading you the Riot Act by then? Make it fifteen."

I clicked off and dialed the pay phone number. Marge answered before the first ring was done.

"You know it's not nice to keep a girl waiting, you jerk." She was trying to tough it out, but I could hear the quaver in her voice.

"I'm sorry, Marge. Things came up."

"Yeah, things came up for me too, two of them with badges. They walked

Fred Adams Jr.

right into my office and demanded to know when I saw you or talked to you last. I said two months ago, so if they catch you, keep the story straight so they don't lock me up along with you."

"Thanks a lot. My day's been fun too."

"I'm sorry, Ike, I'm just scared for you."

"I've been through worse."

We both knew I was lying.

thought about leaving the city, but that would take me away from the heart of things, and no matter how much other people may care for me, how strong their friendship may be, nobody was going to try harder than I would myself.

So long as I was careful and kept my face out of sight, I could walk around Pittsburgh freely. The cops were all looking for that face in the *Press* photo. But they'd be watching my apartment, the office, and my friends pretty close, and that made it tough. Cutter was used to the squeeze; he and I put it on plenty of people when we were on the force, and we knew how it all worked and what to expect. It was Marge I hurt for. I regretted her being dragged into all this.

I hopped a trolley and barely made it to the Iron and Glass Bank on Carson Street before five o'clock. The street lights had begun to wink on in the early dusk. The loose cash in my wallet was running out fast, and I had to break the hundred-dollar bills. The Depression was winding down, but most people still couldn't give you change if you bought a pack of Camels with a C-note.

The Iron and Glass Bank replaced the old Birmingham Hotel that stood on the same spot when I was a kid. The front was all granite and glass, no iron to speak of—go figure— but it was still an impressive building with a big pair of columns flanking the doors. Unlike the double-sized doors you find on court houses and government buildings, designed to intimidate the common people, the Iron and Glass Bank had regular sized doors that made the average Joe feel like he belonged there and wasn't admitted on the sufferance of some giant.

I waited in line at the teller window, and when my turn came, I found myself on the other side of the bars from a dainty little man in a three-piece suit and about four ounces of Brylcreem slicking down hair the color of a phonograph record. He was thumbing through a stack of singles with speed and coordination that would do a card mechanic proud. Finished counting, he tapped the edges of the stack all around, slid a paper band with $100 printed on it over the bundle and put it in his cash drawer. There was my change.

"Yes?" he sniffed, making me feel as if he did me a favor by waiting on me.

"I need to change this bill." I put a hundred down on the marble sill. He started to reach for it, but I kept a finger on it. "You can do that for me. I just saw you put the cash in the drawer."

He eyed the bill as if it were a rare insect, then he eyed me the same way. "Just a moment, please," he said in a voice that would freeze gin. He walked away from the window, and I watched him approach a man in a better suit behind a desk with a name plate that said Erasmus A. Buckley, Assistant Manager. There was some conversation between them and Buckley stood and followed the teller, heels clicking importantly on the marble floor.

I leaned my elbows on the sill, took my face in my hands, and concentrated on Arthur Pennington, steel magnate and eccentric millionaire. By the time the teller and his boss got to the window, the change was complete. "You understand, sir, we have to be careful about accepting large bills. We—"

He got that far before I raised my head and he saw my face, or should I say Arthur Pennington's. His mouth stopped moving. I scowled.

"Oh, good heavens. I didn't realize—" Buckley turned to the confused teller and snapped, "Simpson, do you see who this is?" He wrung his hands. His words tumbled out like rain from a drainpipe. "I'm dreadfully sorry, Mister Pennington. Please understand that we so rarely have to deal with such large bills, and we're always watchful of counterfeit money—oh, not that we'd ever suspect you of such a thing."

If I'd sat my ass on the sill, I have no doubt that the manager would have shoved his lips through the bars and kissed it. "Hmph." I put the second hundred on the counter.

He stared at them and snapped at the teller. "Don't keep Mister Pennington waiting, Simpson," with a voice that threatened the little man's job, if not his life.

Simpson reached under the counter and came up with the banded hundred and a stack of twenties. He counted off five of them and pushed the dough under the grate. I kept my finger on the hundreds for a three count, and Simpson didn't reach for them until I took it away. I put the cash in my pocket and glared one last time at Buckley and Simpson. I'm almost ashamed to say it felt good to make them cringe. Almost.

I walked down Carson watching every person on the sidewalk, in front of me, and behind me in the reflections of the windows of businesses that had closed for the night. It was good I did, because I saw a tan camel-hair overcoat half a block behind me that I'd seen in the lobby of the bank. I stopped to look at a display of neckties in a haberdashery and he stopped too, pretending to be interested in a dark storefront.

I went another block, and he was still on my tail. I was edgy already, but this guy ratcheted things up a notch. I watched him in the glass front of an accountant's office and I made him when he passed a brightly lit deli. Benny Santoro, a small-time numbers runner for the Rubinos. Two-and-two told me he saw me pull a wad of cash out of the bank and he thought I'd be an easy mark.

That's all I need, I thought, and turned into the next alley as if I were taking a Sunday stroll in the park. I hid in a dark doorway and waited. Benny rounded the corner and peered down the alley. He hesitated, but came in anyway, cautious, hanging to the bricks on one side. Good luck for me; it was my side. He passed the doorway, and I saw the shine of a cheap revolver in his hand.

I stepped out behind the dumb *jabroni* and said in his ear, "Hey, Benny." On the second word, I was swinging my sap. It caught him just above his left eye as he turned, and once was enough. His gun clattered on the pavement, and he fell on top of it. I rifled his pockets and found an "Eye-tie roll," a twenty wrapped around thirty or so singles. A lot of flash and not much cash. I shoved it in my pocket. You can never have too much money when you're on the lam.

VII

I spent a good part of the evening in Rocco's, a crowded, noisy, smoky workingman's bar on the east end of Carson that catered to the steel workers who piled in at the end of each shift for the nickel drafts. Like a few others in the Mon Valley, the bar was equipped with a urinal trough that ran its full length so that the hard drinkers wouldn't have to go to the men's room and lose their places. If it offended the two or three floozies in the place, they didn't let on.

I ate a Pittsburgh steak, charred on the outside, pink on the inside. My dad used to work in the J&L mill, and on his lunch break, he'd throw a steak on the red-hot metal of a fresh girder or rail, count to ten, flip it over, give it another ten, and eat it in those big hands of his like some savage in a Tarzan movie. Then he'd come in here after his shift and drink himself into a stupor so I'd have to show up to walk him home, my shoulder in his armpit.

He was too heavy for me to carry up the stairs, so I'd drop him in the middle of the living room floor, and he'd sleep it off 'til noon the next day. Mom, my sisters, and I just stepped over and around him, afraid to wake him up. Work hard, play hard was the Hunky philosophy, and nobody judged. I decided early on that I wasn't going down that road myself and chose instead to be a cop. I hoisted my third draft in a silent salute to his memory. Biggest difference I could see between my old man and me was that I didn't have anybody to carry me home.

I sat in a corner and nobody bothered me. Hell, nobody paid attention to me at all. The big argument at the bar was over who'd win the weekend football game at Forbes Field between the Detroit Lions and the Pirates— the football team, not the baseball team. I was a baseball fan myself, the American Pastime, and I didn't really see what all the fuss was about. I guess it gave them a reason to cheer in the off-season.

Mason came in around half past nine. I waved my hat at him and held up two fingers. He stopped at the bar on his way to the table and brought two foaming mugs of Iron City with him.

"I wish you wouldn't do that," he said, sliding his chair into the table.

"Do what?"

"Look like Roy."

"Sorry." Mason's big brother Elroy, also a cop, was killed in a bank robbery shootout the year after Mason and I joined the force. "I figured you'd find a familiar face easier than you would a strange one. Did anybody follow you?"

"Of course, and I knew I had a tail the whole ride 'til I ran a railroad crossing and they had to stop for a coal train. It was one of those Pennsy freights, probably a mile long. By the time the crossing was clear, I was long gone."

Mason took a long pull on his beer. "Been talking to some people. Word is that somebody high up wants you found pronto. Seems he ain't particular about dead or alive."

"Any idea who that might be?"

"Not yet, but I'm working on it. You need money?"

I told him about Benny Santoro. He laughed. "Too bad you didn't tag him right after he finished collections. You'd be set for a year." He turned his head toward the entrance and slammed down his mug. "Holy hell, it's Czap and Montrose. Quick, you better—" but Mason was talking to the air. I saw them before he did and passed them in the crowd along the bar coming in as I was going out.

Before too long, I'd have to let my face go back to normal. It was starting to ache now, and soon, it would feel like somebody was poking hot needles in it. I was afraid to let it get that far. I could take the hurting, but I wasn't sure what the next step might be. Would it suddenly snap back to my own? Or would it just drift back slowly? Or might it freeze and stay the way it was? Or could it run out of steam halfway like tired muscles and leave my face half mine and half someone else's? Whatever the case, I didn't want to risk finding out.

I needed a place to hole up for the night, but first, I had a visit to make. I decided to walk across the 10th St. bridge back into downtown. It was dark enough that I could let my mug slip back to its natural look for a while. I could feel the tension drain out of my jaw, and the rain that had felt harsh and cold earlier was a cooling relief as it ran down my cheeks.

A trolley clattered past, the roof pole sparking against the overhead cable. In the dim light of the car, I could see people, every one of them with a life of his or her own, a complete story that had nothing to do with me. We all write our own book, I guess, and I was about to write a dark chapter.

Gus "Legs" Legatto ran a pawn shop on Diamond Street, a legit business that fronted for his fencing operation. Unless Billy Cramer changed his m. o. in the last week, his first stop after a haul would be Legatto. The lights were off and the cage was pulled across the front of the store, although there wasn't anything worth breaking the front window to steal; a couple of cheap guitars, a battered saxophone, a wind-up Victrola, mostly junk. The valuables were in the back.

I walked to the end of the block and turned into an alley that led to the back of Legatto's place. It was dim, that eerie never quite dark you find when city lights and the smoldering coke ovens catch the rain or the clouds or the fog and shine overhead with a dull orange glow. Legatto's back door was steel, and looked as if it would stand up to a stick of dynamite.

I crouched behind a row of garbage cans for nearly an hour, waiting and watching. I was about to risk a cigarette, but, a beat cop passed through the alley, checking the door locks. He didn't even look my way. My legs were aching by the time a shadowy figure came down the alley toting a sack, kinda like Santa Claus in reverse.

My patience paid off. The thief rapped on Gus's door; three quick, two slow, three quick. In a minute, a square of light showed through the eye port in the door. It swung open, and in the light, I could make out Ollie Bryner, a small-time burglar and Gus, all three hundred pounds of him, gut pushing through a vest he could no longer button. Bryner stepped inside, and the door closed.

Bryner came out a half hour later without his bag. He looked one way then the other and scurried around the corner before the beat cop could catch him and shake him down for his take. I counted to a hundred then came out of hiding. I took a deep breath and concentrated on Gino Patricelli, a burglar on the same rung of the crime ladder as Bryner. My face ached a little as I made the shift, but it didn't hurt for long.

I used the secret knock; three quick, two slow, three quick. Nobody came. I knocked again, a little harder. The eye port slid open and Gus peered out. I turned my face so he could see it. "You again? Must be a good night." The eye port closed, and I heard the snick of two bolts sliding open. The door swung inward, Gus holding it in one hand as he gestured with the other. "Right this way."

He closed the door behind me, and as he slid the bolts to, I put my face back. Time to start the party.

"Whattaya got? No sack?"

I turned, he saw my face, and his mouth fell open. I hit him with an uppercut and it slammed shut again. He staggered back a step but didn't fall. I gave him a hard shot just over his belt. That gut of his wasn't built for punishment. He doubled over, but I saw his hand reach into his trouser pocket. I cracked his wrist with my sap and a little revolver fell to the floor. I kicked it away and backhanded the sap across the side of his head, not hard enough to knock him out—I wanted him awake and aware—just enough for him to see stars.

I grabbed him by his hair and dragged him stumbling into the room behind the shop. I threw him into a chair that almost collapsed under his weight and clamped one of my mitts around his chin. His little dark eyes showed some white as I pulled back the sap for another hit.

"Mars," he stammered, "what the hell—"

"You and I are going to have a little talk, Gus. If I like what you tell me, I won't have to use this." I jerked my head at the sap. "Now, fat boy, tell me about Billy Cramer." I couldn't swear to it, but his eyes got just a little bit wider.

"Cramer? He—he's dead."

"And I bet you know why."

"I don't know nothing."

"Wrong answer." I brought the sap down on his kneecap. Gus gritted his teeth and grunted in pain. "Billy came to see you in the last week with a score, didn't he?" I raised the sap over his other knee. "Didn't he?"

"Yeah, he was here. He brought in some stuff."

"What kind of stuff?"

"The usual; just some jewelry, a pocket watch, a diamond ring. You know."

"And that's all?"

He nodded so fast I thought his head had come loose. "Yeah, that's it."

I cracked his other knee. Gus screamed this time."Try again, Gus."

"Jesus! Stop it." Tears were dripping off his jowls. "I'll talk. I'll talk."

"I know you will, you fat toad." I tapped the blackjack on the bridge of his nose, suggesting my next target. "Tell me about the key."

Pay dirt. Mason calls the look Gus gave me "eyes of prey," that look that a trapped animal gets when it can't run and it knows it can't win the fight. "They'll kill me if I tell you."

"I'll kill you now if you don't. Tell me and you might live long enough to run for it."

"Cramer handed over the jewelry and then he said, 'I got something else, Gus, but I don't know what to do with it.'"

I wanted to say "the key," but I didn't want to lead him into saying what I wanted to hear. "Tell me about it."

"It was a key with a square head. He said he found it with the other stuff in a lockbox. He couldn't figure what it was for, but he said it must be important to be locked up with the valuables."

"And?"

"Between the two of us we thought we could sell it back, kinda like ransom."

I nodded slowly. "Makes sense so far, Gus. Now tell me, who did Billy Cramer steal it from?"

"You won't believe me if I tell you."

"Try me."

"Ambrose Jeffers, the D.A."

"You're right, I don't believe you."

"I'll prove it to you. In the safe."

I put my sap back in my pocket and took out my .38. "All right, Gus. Let's go. No tricks or you'll die slow and painful." I hauled him out of the chair and held him by the back of his collar as he limped to the safe, an old Acme whose wheels rested on squares of thick wood. Why are they always black?

Gus knelt and started turning the dial.

"Got a gun in there, Gus?" I put the muzzle of my pistol in the corner of his eye. He didn't answer, so I cocked the hammer.

"Yeah, I got a gun in there."

"Is it loaded?"

He nodded.

"Open the safe, reach in, and take it out by the barrel. Thumb and forefinger."

His stubby sausage fingers worked the dial. I heard the tumblers click, and he pulled down the handle.

"Slow."

He swung the door open and reached inside. His hand came out with a big Webley revolver.

"Throw it away." Gus tossed the pistol aside and it clattered into a corner. "Now the proof."

Gus pulled out a steel lockbox the size of a brick. I could see it had been jimmied; the lid was bent over the lock. The hinges were sprung, and they squeaked as Gus raised the lid. He reached in and pulled out a gold pocket watch on a chain. He pressed the stem, and the lid flipped open. "There. There's your proof." He handed me the watch.

Engraved on the inside of the case were the words: Ambrose Jeffers, in recognition of your public service, January 14, 1937—The Greater Pittsburgh Chamber of Commerce.

"And I guarantee you," Gus said, "he's one person don't need to hock anything."

I shoved Gus and he sprawled on the floor sideways. The box spilled, scattering jewelry across the floor. "But you got greedy, didn't you, Gus? You decided to run your own game and look for other bidders."

He was quiet for a three count. "Yeah, I mighta put the word out on the street that I had something big for the right price." He rolled back upright. "But nobody bit."

"They didn't have to, you dumb shit. It doesn't take Steinmetz to add it up. If I figured it out, other people have too. And for that matter, even the

D.A.'s office has ears in the wall." I shook my head. "Dumb."

I should have asked Gus if he had two guns in the safe. He reached in and came up with a two-barrel Derringer and managed to fire one shot that took a piece off my ear before I put one through his eye and out the back of his head. Like I said, Dumb. And dead.

I dropped Jeffers' watch in my pocket and stepped over the minor mountain of Gus's corpse. On the surface, it would look like a robbery gone bad, or maybe just a falling out among thieves. As an afterthought, I rifled Gus's pockets for his keys and in the bargain found a thick roll of bills that had fewer ones than twenties. I figured he wouldn't need it, or the stack in the safe either.

I slipped out the steel door into the alley and locked up after myself. I threw Gus's keys into one of the garbage cans, and in two minutes, I was on a trolley heading for Manchester.

Things made a little more sense now. Whatever the key kept locked up, it was big; big money, or maybe big evidence on somebody, or, knowing Jeffers, a lot of big somebodies. Big enough to get a lot of people killed. Jeffers knows what it is. Billy Cramer steals the key and he and Gus try to squeeze Jeffers for it. He arranges for Cramer to hand it off to Kobylarz and Watts, but some other players who want the key tumble to the meeting and shoot him. Billy gets away and hands me the key. The flatfeet brace me for it, but I get away. Then they turn up dead, and I turn up on the front page of the *Sun-Telegraph*.

I could go to Czap, tell him the whole tale, but with Jeffers involved, I wouldn't have much chance to see Christmas. And for that matter, I'd probably get George killed in the bargain. My best hope was to find the lock that the Key fit. That's how I'd started to think of it, with a capital K, as if it were the only key in the world.

Lockie said it was the key to a car, maybe a Hudson, but where would I start looking for a Hudson? I couldn't just walk up and down the street looking for Hudsons and ring the doorbell and tell the householder, "Pardon me, sir, but could I please try this key in the trunk of your car?" If it was the right Hudson, he'd probably blow my head off.

There were hundreds of them in the city alone, and unlike a building that just sits there, cars roll anywhere and everywhere. My guess was, though, that it was close enough so that Jeffers could get to it easily. So, I started thinking like a detective instead of Raymond Chandler. How many Hudsons in Pittsburgh? Who would know? The Bureau of Motor Vehicles might be able to tell me, but since I lost my cop status, they don't take my calls anymore. Besides, for them to sift through tens of thousands of registrations to isolate one make of car in one city would take weeks, once they got around to it.

My best bet was Warner Motors, the Hudson dealer on the North Shore in the Mexican War Streets. A quick glam at their sales records would tell me who bought a Hudson and when. Of course, that was assuming the Hudson was bought new and not used, or stolen. After all, I was dealing with crooks. I looked at my watch. Still too early for a break-in; I'd have to wait for the small hours before trying that stunt.

The trolley stopped at an intersection, and a uniformed cop got on. I turned my head, looking out the window, and hoped he didn't make me. I was lucky; he knew the trolleyman and sat up front, chatting with him 'til he got off four blocks later—without paying, I might add. Perks of the badge.

I stepped off the trolley and back into the rain. The Mexican War district was close by, a group of streets named after Generals in the war: Fremont Street, Sherman Avenue, and Taylor Avenue; and their big battles: Buena Vista Street, Palo Alto Street, and Resaca Place. I took my time, strolling along the rows of brick town houses, built when business was better and cash was flowing freely.

Warner Motors was close by on Sampsonia Way, next to the Stearns and Foster Mattress warehouse. I walked past the building. It was two floors with big single-pane display windows showing four new cars on the ground floor. People who bought Hudsons didn't like to kick tires in the rain or snow.

I stood on the sidewalk, looking in, as if I was admiring the new Silver Terraplane convertible. Hudsons had gotten away from the shoebox Model A look and like most American cars, they were aping the sleek curves of the Cord. I imagined the straight eight under that long hood and what it would feel like to open it up on a good stretch of road with Marge beside me, going anywhere; it didn't matter where.

At the back of the first floor I saw a few desks, probably for the salesmen, and a door leading to the rear half of the building; offices, service bays, and the ramp to the second floor where they kept their stock. I strolled on,

My best bet was Warner Motors...

two blocks before I doubled back down the alley. The rear of the Warner Motors Building had a pair of pull-up garage doors for the service area and one regular door to the right.

I cupped a match in my hand and studied the lock. It was a Yale. Child's play. I looked around the door area and found what I expected, a Detex watchman's key station. Under the metal flap was a key on a chain. The watchman used a unique key for each station on his rounds to punch the clock he carried on a strap over his shoulder. They didn't need one out front because of the lights. My guess was they shared a night watchman with the mattress warehouse and other businesses on the street.

I settled down in the shadows and waited, hoping the watchman would come past soon. I was lucky; I was only half soaked when I saw the flashlight bobbing down the alley. He was a tall guy, skinny. Couldn't guess his age, but he walked with a limp like he had a bad hip. He punched his clock, closed the key flap and went on his way down the block. I thought about waiting for him to come by again to know the frequency of his rounds, but I was just too wet and too cold.

It took me all of twelve seconds to pick the lock. There was no McClintock alarm box on the outside wall, so I figured it was safe to open the door and go inside.

The offices were to the right of the service area. I found a filing cabinet in the second one with drawers labeled Sales by Year. I pulled out the drawer for 1934. The Depression slowed things down for the average Joe, but not for the better off. Warner Motors sold more Hudsons that year than I would have guessed. I held a penlight in my teeth and jotted down the names. I could get the addresses from a phone book later. Next, 1935. Another good year for Warner. Halfway through the files, I saw a name that gave me a start. I was expecting Jeffers, but who I found was even more interesting: Francis McNairy.

Irish Frank was currently doing ten to twenty for a jewel heist in the lobby of the Clark Building on Liberty Avenue, home of a cabal of jewelers and the Pittsburgh Diamond Exchange. I was off duty that day and missed the whole thing, but the story was a regular topic for years after.

A courier heading for the Diamond Exchange on the sixth floor got in the elevator and when the doors closed, he was looking down the barrel of a gun. The operator was McNairy in a stolen uniform. He took the courier to the basement where his two partners were waiting. They cut the handcuff off the bag with bolt cutters, slugged the courier, and took off. Their big mistake was not shooting him.

Unfortunately for them, the yegg who hit the courier didn't hit him quite hard enough. He pretended to be out, and watched as the hoods shoved his pouch into an alligator briefcase and McNairy changed into a business suit. They got back on the elevator, and as soon as they did, the courier went to the fuse box and threw the master switch, shutting off the power to the building. Then he ran out into the street to the first cop he saw.

By the time McNairy and his partners climbed out of the elevator's emergency hatch and got out of the shaft, the heat was on the way. They were smart enough to split up; they had three different cars waiting. Witnesses said McNairy ran out of the building carrying the alligator briefcase. A getaway car pulled up and Frank jumped in. Can you guess the make and model? A two-tone, black-on-silver Hudson Terraplane coupe.

He traded a few shots with the cops who came running. Too bad for them they brought brogans to an auto race. McNairy's wheel man roared off like Barney Oldfield and disappeared across the Sixth Street Bridge. By the time roadblocks were set up, McNairy had escaped the net; same with his pals. One hundred G's, give or take, in diamonds. McNairy's accomplices were never found, or identified. McNairy's car was never found, either, but McNairy was.

He made the mistake of jilting his girlfriend. A stripper at the old Harris Theater on Forbes, renamed the Casino when George Jaffe bought it a few years back. A month or so after the heist, he gave her the gate for another broad just like her, and she did what any self-respecting woman would do. She told the cops where to find him.

The cops broke down the door of his hideout and caught him with his new squeeze, but no jewels. The prosecutor on the case: Assistant District Attorney Ambrose Jeffers. McNairy was positively I.D.'d by the courier, and he went to the slammer, never blowing the whistle on his helpers and never breathing a word about the car.

For the sake of thoroughness, I jotted down the remaining names in the file, closed the drawer, wiped off my prints, and left the way I came. The alley door gave me trouble relocking it, and I was so cold and wet and tired that I just left it unlatched. By the time the watchman came around again and found the unlocked door, I'd be across the river with one more piece of the puzzle.

IX

I never doubted for a second that Ambrose Jeffers was crooked. I mean, he's a Pittsburgh politician, right? He had access to all the info on the Clark heist, including evidence in the case. The cops tried to sweat McNairy as to where he stashed the jewels, but no dice. McNairy wouldn't spill it. But maybe Jeffers was savvy enough to swipe the key from evidence and hang onto it for future reference. Find the car, find the diamonds. Now I had the key, and it was my job.

I considered getting out of town. If I did, I wouldn't be able to work to clear myself. With somebody else's face, I could breeze right past the cops to the ticket window and buy a train ride to Pismo Beach if I wanted to, but here was where I'd clear myself.

I had a really perverse idea to shake things up. The penny arcade on Penn had one of those four for a dime photo booths. I sat down in it and pulled the curtain. I pulled my hat down low. held up the key in one hand and the watch in the other, and dropped my dime in the slot. Four flashes, and in a minute, four snapshots scrolled out in a sepia and white strip. As soon as I found a stamp and an envelope, one of them would be on its way to Jeffers . I didn't know if it would help my cause any, but it would be satisfying to imagine him sweating when he realized somebody breathing had the damned key and connected him to it.

I pulled a leaf out of my notebook and scrawled a quick note to Marge on it. It read: need all you can find about Irish Frank McNairy, especially before the Clark heist; family, background, anything. Talk to you same time, same station. Marge's apartment was a few blocks from the intersection where I got off the trolley.

I walked to Algonquin Street and down the block about fifty feet from Marge's building, I saw what had to be an unmarked car. Some of these guys ought to just paint COP on the doors in three-foot letters. It'd be more subtle. On the street beside the sedan were at least ten cigarette butts. They teach us to look for that as a sign of a getaway car in a bank robbery. You'd think that cops on stake out would remember. Maybe they think they're too smart to be seen.

A few seconds behind a tree, and I looked like my barber, Eddie. I climbed the steps to the doorway with a cigarette in my mouth. I turned when I opened the door and threw it away. They got a good look at me in the vestibule light and convinced themselves I wasn't their target. Then I saw the second car parked on the same side of the street but about thirty feet back. The lights from a passing car showed me two heads in the front.

I was important to the cops, but not so important they'd put two cars on the same stake out. The Department budget has limits, after all. It looked as if somebody else was interested in talking to me. I went inside and punched the up button for the elevator. The kid running the car didn't pay me any more mind than he would any other stranger.

I got off on seven and was relieved to see nobody outside Marge's apartment. I waited 'til the elevator left and stepped up to the door. I slipped the note under it and knocked, then I zipped down the hall like some kid on a Halloween prank. I took the stairs down, and I took my time about it. I wanted to see Marge more than I want to admit, but I couldn't risk putting her in danger.

The elevator bell dinged as I stepped out of the stairwell. The doors opened, and Marge got out. "Hey, Eddie," she called. "Long time no see." Before I could speak, she crossed the foyer and took me by the hand. "Wanna come up for a drink?" Then she whispered under her breath, "Or do you want me punch you right in the nose?"

I nodded. "Yeah, sure. Sounds like fun." She put her arm in mine and steered me back to the elevator. "Going up, Wilbur."

"Sure thing, Miss Conway." The elevator boy leered at her double *entendre*—that's another one she taught me—and pulled the cage across the car.

As soon as we got in the apartment, she snapped. "If you want me to kiss you, get rid of that stupid barber's face."

I did, and she did, and that kept up, with some variation, 'til we both fell asleep in her big brass bed.

woke up to the sound of scratching, very faint, coming from the living room. I held my breath and listened. Someone was picking the lock. I shook Marge gently and clamped a hand over her mouth. She started awake, and I whispered in her ear, "Get in the closet. Don't make any noise." She nodded and I took my hand away.

I slipped out of bed and put on my pants and my holster. If it was the cops, they'd kick the door down, not pick the lock like a burglar. I didn't want to use my gun because that would bring the guys from the stakeout running, and even if I got away, they'd arrest Marge for hiding me. This had to be handled quietly.

I tiptoed into the darkened living room; I knew where the furniture was, so I didn't trip over anything. I stood just to the side of the doorway, barely breathing. Whoever was picking the lock wasn't as good as he should be. I got tired of waiting and almost opened the door for him just to get things rolling.

Finally, the lock clicked, and a line of light appeared at the edge of the door. It pushed in two inches and stopped. The chain was on, so they couldn't just sashay in. I saw a curved piece of wire snake around the door and hook the chain. A little finagling, and the end of the chain slipped out of the track. At least the guy was smart enough to let it down easy and not make any noise.

The door opened a few inches more. A hand with a pistol came through it. What happened next was pure reflex on my part. I threw my whole two hundred pounds against the door and heard bones crunch in his wrist. He dropped the gun. I grabbed his forearm and yanked him through the doorway, clubbing him across the back of his head with my sap.

As I did, I saw his partner in the hallway reaching for his piece as he came through the doorway. I swung the sap backhand and hit him right between the eyes. He staggered back and I grabbed him by his coat. I rammed his head into the doorjamb a couple of times, and he dropped to the floor.

Now what?

Nothing moved in the hallway; no doors opened, no curious heads popped out. Of course not; it was four a.m. Respectable people were in bed asleep like I was a few minutes ago. I dragged the second hood into the living room and closed the door. I switched on the light.

One of the hoods I recognized as Nick LaSorda. His partner looked familiar, but I couldn't remember his name. The first thing I did after I smacked them again to make sure they stayed down, was take their guns. Then I tied their hands with the cords from Marge's end table lamps. I'd've tied their feet too, but I ran out of lamps and I didn't want to pull the telephone wire out of the wall.

A quick rifling of their pockets pulled up wallets. I was right about LaSorda. His partner was William Vanner. I'd heard his name on the street, but we'd never met. LaSorda was a low-rent leg breaker for a couple of the local shylocks. I figured Vanner was on the same rung of the ladder, birds of a feather and all that.

Then I remembered Marge. I went back into the bedroom and said. "All clear. You can come out now."

I opened the closet door and found myself staring down the muzzle of the purse-sized .32 automatic I gave Marge for her birthday last year. She stared over the sight, wide eyed, holding the pistol in both hands like Edward Van Sloan holding the cross in Bela Lugosi's face in *Dracula*.

She relaxed when she saw it was me and put down the pistol. "God, Mars, I heard some banging around, then I didn't hear anything for five minutes, and I thought—"

I put my fingertips against her lips. "It's all okay, Marge, but I've got to think fast."

She sat on the bed and I sat beside her. I put an arm around her shoulders. "I'm sorry I put you in the middle of all this."

She shook her head. "Don't be. It's a story I can tell my grandchildren someday, if I ever have any."

"I have an idea."

I went back out into the living room and pulled LaSorda into a sitting position. I punched him in the mouth and felt a few teeth give. His lip split, and blood oozed down his chin. I rolled Vanner over and stiff armed his nose.

"What the hell are you doing, Mars?" It was a good sign that she was calling me by my last name again. Marge was drifting back to normal.

"You'll see." I dragged the two gunsels out into the hall and down the fire stairs one at a time. I left them on the landing of the sixth floor, untied, and sprawling. As an extra touch, I poured a little of the gin from the bottle in Marge's kitchen cabinet on them.

Back upstairs, I dialed the precinct. "Police. Schiller."

"This is the building super in the Royal Apartments over on Algonquin. I've got two guys fighting in the stairway. Sounds like they're killing each other. Send somebody would you?" I hung up before the desk sergeant could respond.

I pushed a wad of bills into Marge's hand. "Tomorrow, go to work like normal, and when you go to lunch, buy an overnight bag. After work, go to the Ritz-Carlton and check in under the name Mary Smith. I'll call you there."

"But my things . . ."

"We'll worry about that later. You can't come back here right now, and we can't let on to the cops that anything's wrong. People are looking to get at me through you, and you have to disappear for a day or two 'til this is all over."

"I have to go now. Cops'll be all over the building in a few minutes, and I don't want to push my luck." I kissed her and kissed her once more for good measure. Then I rang for the elevator. I almost forgot to put Eddie's face back on before the doors opened. Wilbur was still on duty, and he gave me a smirk as I got on. I wanted to punch him on general principles. Maybe later.

The elevator landed in the lobby, and as the doors opened, I saw two men run through the entrance doors. Snaith and Wilcosky, the stakeout cops. They would have heard the dispatch call. The pair gave me a passing glance as they ran by to the fire stairs. I walked out of the lobby twirling Lasorda's keys around my finger.

His car was pretty nice, a '37 Packard with a good heater and an even better radio. As I drove down Algonquin, I saw the spinners on a prowl car coming the other way.

The cops would put LaSorda and Vanner on ice for a day or two; drunk and disorderly at the least. Assault for one or the other or both. Maybe trespassing. Maybe more if I was lucky. No way on the planet would they tell the cops they were there to terrorize Marge. And when they got out of the cage, I figured they wouldn't report the Packard stolen, either. They'd want to find it themselves.

I took 19 out of town and pulled off the road at an all-night diner outside Canonsburg. I used a dime to unscrew the license plate from the Packard and switch it with an old Model A parked beside me. I put my hat over my eyes and leaned back in the seat. It would be a few hours before Art McCurdy got to his shop.

XI

I pulled in front of Canonsburg Auto Repair at eight o'clock just as Art McCurdy was unlocking the door. McCurdy could have made two of me, maybe two and a half. He was a couple of inches taller and a couple of feet wider. His head looked small on his shoulders, and instead of a neck, a pyramid of fat connected it to his shoulders.

McCurdy was out of the "baby" business, barely escaping jail the last time he repainted a boosted car, but he owed me big for rescuing his teenaged daughter two years ago when a couple of white slavers shanghaied her and pressed her into the trade. We never talked about what happened next, or the final disposition of the two pimps, but it was understood that if I ever needed help, he was first in line—and second.

Art did a double take when he saw me get out of the car. "Jesus Christ." He opened the door and waved me in. "Get in here quick, before somebody sees you."

"Hi, Art."

"Mars." His eyes darted around behind his glasses like he expected a swarm of cops to descend any second and he was looking for an escape hatch.

"How's Jenny doing these days?"

"She started nursing school two months ago. She's doing okay."

"Glad to hear it. How about Ethel?"

"She's okay too." Neither of us spoke for a good minute. Art took a paper sack of Mail Pouch from his pocket and pulled out a wad of tobacco. He put it in his cheek like a squirrel with a nut.

"You're famous, Mars."

"Even out here in the sticks?"

"We get the Pittsburgh papers every day, believe it or not, and you've been on the front page the last two of them."

"Don't believe everything you read."

"I don't, or we wouldn't be having this conversation."

"I need your special skills."

"I figured. Is it hot?"

"Depends on your definition. When you steal from a thief, what do you call it?"

"I call it comeuppance."

"Glad we agree."

Art pulled up the door to his painting bay and I pulled the Packard inside.

"That's Centennial Blue on it now," Art said. "I almost hate to change the color, it looks so nice."

"How about red?"

He shook his head." Nope. They don't paint Packards that color. At least they didn't in '37. I paint it red, I might as well paint the word 'stolen' on the trunk."

"What do you think would be good?"

He stood for a minute chewing his cud then said, "Indian Maroon," with a curt nod. "I can match the factory paint well enough it'd fool a dealer, and I won't need as many coats as I would painting it Buckingham Grey or Packard Cream."

"Can I hole up here while you do the job?"

"Sure. I can't exactly say 'make yourself comfortable' back there in the storeroom, but you're welcome to it."

I found an empty corner of the storeroom and sat with my back to the wall. In a few minutes I nodded off to the rattling of the air compressor.

Art kicked my foot with the toe of his boot. "It's done. Not my finest work, on such a short clock, but it'll get by."

I looked at my watch. I'd been asleep for four hours. I stood up and stretched, my hands at the small of my back. "Let's take a look."

The car looked not only brand new, but on close inspection, I saw no hints that it had been repainted, no overspray on the glass, tires, or chrome.

"It's a masterpiece." I pulled out my roll and started peeling off bills. Art put up his hand. "I'm not taking a dime for this. And I won't next time either."

"How about the third?" He shook his head.

As I drove away, I decided that I'd find out how much tuition cost for nursing school, put it in an envelope, and send it—no name—to Ethel.

Rolling out of Canonsburg, I flinched when I saw a patrol car in my rear-view mirror. I stopped at a stop sign and rolled down the window to stick out my arm and signal a right turn to see if he'd follow me. As I was doing that, the spinner lit up on the cop's roof and he hit the siren. My hand went into my jacket and closed on the handle of my pistol.

The cop car shot around me, ran the stop sign and took off down the street. I let out the long breath I'd been holding and counted my blessings. A horn blared behind me. I looked in the mirror and saw a dark sedan with some fat guy in a hat behind the wheel. "Move it, you stupid son of a bitch," he yelled. Some days I might have gotten out of the car and rearranged his face for him, but today, I had to keep a low profile.

I made the turn and drove two blocks before I went back to Route 19. Instead of going North back to Pittsburgh, I headed South to Washington. I needed to just sit for a while and think without feeling the need to look over my shoulder every ten seconds. I needed a bed, a bathtub, a telephone, and a newspaper, and the likeliest place I could find all four was the George Washington Hotel.

The GW, as the locals call it, was an ambitious hotel for a city that size, ten stories and two hundred rooms, but in the Twenties when business was booming, it seemed like a good idea. But before I checked into the joint, I needed a suitcase.

Nothing attracts the attention of a hotel detective like a guest with no luggage. I drove around the back streets of town and found a second-hand shop with a sign in the window: Motley Odds: If we don't have it, you don't need it.

I put on Mason's face and climbed out of the car. A light drizzle had started again, and the water beaded up on the Packard's new paint like rivets on a girder. The car looked good, and I felt safe driving it.

The front window of Motley Odds was so full of merchandise that I could barely see inside. I stepped in out of the rain, and into a jumble of everything imaginable piled floor to ceiling in a rat's maze of aisles. A spare tire and an eye-stalk headlight from an old Ford shared a battered dining table with a gaudy kewpie doll lamp, an old mandolin, a set of encyclopedias and two meat cleavers. Shelves made of planks across bricks held glassware and bric-a-brac stacked to the stamped tin ceiling. Another mound of stuff included an old Army canteen, a hammer with one claw broken off, a red railroad lantern, a toy train and track sticking haphazardly out of an orange crate, and an open purple silk parasol.

"You need an umbrella, right?"

I turned and saw a man who looked like he could give Methuselah a run for his money. He was maybe four-foot nine, and ninety pounds but looked like he used to be six foot one and two hundred, then he shrunk but his skin didn't. Instead, it folded into the deepest set of wrinkles I've ever seen. But the green eyes under a full head of white hair shone like a school boy's. He talked around a crinkled cigarette that burned dangerously close to setting his bushy moustache on fire.

"Or maybe you need a raincoat."

I shook my head. "No, I need a suitcase."

"A man on the move, eh? Well, let's see what we can find that'll 'suit' your case." He chuckled at his own joke and waved for me to follow him. Near the back of his store was a pile of old luggage that looked as if some red cap had spilled a baggage cart in the corner. He bent over and dug through the heap of suitcases and valises, throwing them to either side. He straightened up with a tan leather one-suiter that had buckled straps to hold it shut.

He held it in front of him like a shield. "Now here's a fine piece of workmanship." I noticed that his left hand was holding a corner whose stitching had come out so it wouldn't gap open. "Fifty cents."

"Okay," I said, digging in my pocket for the coins.

"You ain't gonna dicker?"

"No, fifty cents sounds about right."

He frowned. "You take all the fun out of it. But don't worry, I won't tell."
I started in spite of myself. "Tell who?"

"Whoever's looking for you," he cackled. "Angry wife, angry husband, process server. If you had the time, I bet you'd'a dickered with me. If they come in here after you I'll just tell 'em, 'Ain't seen the fellow.'"

He took the half dollar from me, jingled the coins in his palm, and shoved them into the pocket of his baggy trousers. He walked away cackling, "Nope, won't tell a soul." He was still talking to himself when I went out the door.

I was feeling pretty confident up to that point that I was slipping past everybody unnoticed, but the old man spooked me. Maybe I was just worn out. I couldn't get a room and get off the street fast enough.

The lobby of the George Washington Hotel was slow that time of day, and as I walked up to the wrap-around counter, the clerk took his time shuffling some papers and looking in the pigeon holes for keys and messages. A bellhop in a dark green uniform leaned against the end of the counter and made no offer to take my suitcase. Maybe they hoped I'd go away, since I didn't look like their usual clientele. Granted, I was in day old clothes and needed a shave and a bath, but my money was green.

While I waited for the clerk to pretend he finally noticed me, I looked around. Any one of the big empty leather armchairs in the lobby would have cost a month's rent for my office and two for my apartment. The teardrop chandelier looked like it took a month to clean.

The clerk finally couldn't stall any more. He had to either wait on me or tell me to get lost. I figured I could probably break the bony bastard in half over my knee if I wanted to. His slicked back hair and skinny moustache made him look like a shoe salesman in some Spencer Tracy comedy. "May I help you?" His voice was as oily as his hair.

"A room with a bath for one night."

He eyed me up and down and paused for a second or two on my suitcase. He sniffed, "All of our rooms have baths."

"Then I want one for tonight."

"That will be thirty dollars." He paused for emphasis. "In advance."

That was steep, and I wondered if he grabbed the price out of the air or it was management policy to deter potential customers who didn't suit the GW's image. They probably charged the Rockefellers twelve—and grabbed their luggage on the sidewalk.

What I wanted to do was grab the clerk by his necktie, haul him over the counter and knock out a few of his teeth. What I did was pull out my roll and count out the money. He made it a point to recount the bills and with a disapproving frown, rotated the register toward me on its lazy Susan platform. Coming off the Depression, even a ritzy joint like the GW couldn't turn down cash with a good conscience.

I signed as Mason Cutter, Pittsburgh, Pennsylvania and turned the register back toward him.

"Checkout is eleven o'clock," the clerk said, scrutinizing my signature, "Mister Cutter. Otherwise, you'll be charged for an additional day."

I nodded. "I understand." If I didn't have things to do and places to go, I would have waited 'til ten fifty-nine to hand in my key, just to disappoint the creep.

He set a key on a fob that said 317 on the counter but kept his hand on it. He stood a moment longer, looking at me as if I were a dog turd on the sidewalk. The clerk rang the brass service bell on the counter and snapped, "Front," even though the bellhop was only twenty feet away and was watching the whole scene.

The bellhop scurried over and took the key. I guess he saw my roll when I paid for the room and figured on a healthy tip. I beat him to the suitcase. I didn't want him to carry it, but not because I was being stingy or mean; he'd figure out it was empty in two seconds, and that would buy me a close eye from the hotel dick.

I followed him to the elevator. He closed the cage and we started up. On closer inspection, I realized he was no kid. My guess was thirty-five, and he had that tired look of people who scrape out a living wearing uniforms and being deferential to folks with money, trading a little piece of self-respect for every tip, and seeing nothing different on the horizon. One more reason I liked being my own boss, although I had to admit, that day the quiet life had a certain attraction.

"Ever get a call for Philip Morris?"

He laughed. "I wish just once I did."

We got to the third floor and he opened the cage on an empty corridor. The George Washington had that eerie quiet big hotels cultivate that makes you feel as if that everybody else on the planet died and you're the last one left.

We stepped off the elevator and I followed the bellhop down the thick maroon tongue of carpet to 317. He unlocked the door. It swung inside, and he stepped back to let me go in first. "There you are."

The room was nice, a lot nicer than my apartment and miles past the Mingott.

"That will be thirty dollars." He paused for emphasis. "In advance."

"If you need anything else, Mister Cutter, just ring the desk and ask for me." He was sharp; the clerk said my name only once, but he picked it up and remembered it.

"What's your name?"

"Albert."

I held out my hand to shake. "Mason."

He shook my hand but looked surprised. "Pleased to meet you."

"There is one thing you could do for me, Albert."

"Sure."

I handed him a five-dollar bill. "Get me a copy of today's *Pittsburgh Press* or the *Sun-Telegraph* from the newsstand up the street and bring it up. And a pint of bourbon. Keep the change."

"Gee, thanks." He hesitated at the door. "We don't like him either."

"Who?"

"Robert the desk clerk. He thinks because he wears a suit and we wear these dopey uniforms that he's better than we are."

"A suit's just another uniform, Albert, just another uniform."

XII

Speaking of suits, I figured I should probably get another outfit. It was cold weather, but these clothes would start to smell in another day or so. Albert was back with a copy of both newspapers in a few minutes, so I ran as hot a bath as I could stand and soaked in it while I read the news.

I was still on page one, but under the fold now. The Press said I was "still at-large." I could imagine Marge with her blue pencil editing the article. I asked her once if she knew where "at-large" came from. She said France. In French *au large* means "at liberty." Makes sense. And as long as my luck and my nerve held out, that's where I'd be: at liberty.

The water went lukewarm, and I tripped the drain with my toe. The tub ran almost empty, and I started all over again, refilling it with steaming water. I had let my looks slip back to normal after Albert brought the papers, and now I laid back in the tub and draped a hot washcloth over my face.

The muscles hurt. I had swapped faces more often in the last two days than I had the last six months, and held them for a longer time. The hot water soaked into my skin, and it carried the warmth deep into my face, Soon, I was snoring.

When I woke up, the washcloth had gone cold, and the bath was on the way. I hauled myself out of the tub and wrapped myself in one of the big fluffy bath towels hanging on the rack. Maybe the place was worth thirty a day. A table-sized Zenith radio stood on the night stand beside the telephone. I switched it on while I toweled myself off. The last person in the room had dialed the radio to a station that was broadcasting a Bible-thumping evangelist who pronounced Jesus "Jay-zis" and told me I was going to burn in hell if I didn't seek redemption.

I was more interested in a new suit, a thick steak, and a stiff drink. I switched off the radio.

Main Street in Washington, Pennsylvania had three men's clothing stores with suits and neckties in their front windows. I picked Gabriel's because when I looked through the front glass, I saw one person in the whole place. It looked to be the least busy and the likeliest to take care of me on the quick.

I walked in and immediately a little man in a three-piece suit hurried over. He eyed me like a cat eyeing a mouse. "Hello, sir, can I help you?"

"I need a suit."

He nodded confidently. "Suits, I got." He stuck out his hand. "Solomon Gabriel. Call me Sol."

"Mason Cutter."

His handshake was strong for a little guy. He took me by the elbow and led me to the back of the store where the suits hung on racks like rows of unemployed stockbrokers in a bread line.

"Slow day today?" I asked, looking around.

Sol laughed. "You're here today, so, no." He stood back and held up his thumb like an artist, sizing me up and comparing me to a couple of mannequins. "I make you for a forty-two long. Sound right?"

"I haven't bought a suit for a while, so I can't say."

He went to a rack and pulled two navy blue suits on hangers. "You like single-breasted or double-breasted?" He held up one of each.

"Uh, single." I always laugh when I see the tough guys in gangster movies wearing double-breasted suits. A double-breasted coat can slow you down big time if you're wearing a shoulder rig, and they're impossible if you wear a cross-draw holster.

"Single it is." Sol put the double-wide away and brought the other suit over. Up close I could see it wasn't just navy blue, it had a fine grey pinstripe in the weave. He took the coat by the collar and pulled it upward off the hanger like a magician unveiling the goldfish swimming in a previously empty bowl. "Try this for size."

I shucked off my jacket and he saw my gun. "You wear that every day?" He asked me matter-of-factly, like he was asking me whether I knotted my necktie with a single or a double Windsor knot.

"Yeah. I'm a private detective."

"Didn't ask, my friend." He looked at the coat, my .38, and the coat again and nodded his head. "I can ease the underarm a little and you'll never know it's there."

Sol had a good eye. I slipped on the coat and it was a good fit across the shoulders and chest. The sleeves were a little long, but close enough.

"Now the trousers." I changed into the suit pants in a little curtained dressing room and came out to find Sol in his vest with a tape measure over his shoulders like Father Janos's surplice and a mouthful of pins. He stood me on a drum-shaped riser like a lion tamer might use in the circus. The trousers were a little loose in the waist, but Sol assured me that would be no problem.

The cuffs dragged the ground behind my heels and crowned across the arch of my shoe. "That I can fix," he said around the pins, dropping to one knee and marking the inseam with a piece of tailor's chalk.

When he finished fussing around the legs, I stepped down from the riser. "The reason I asked about how busy you are is that I need the suit in a hurry." I held up a fifty from Gus's safe. He took it and smiled.

"I had to let my tailor go," he said with a little shrug. "But I can do the job myself, though. Did it for years before I opened this place." He walked to the front door and turned the Open sign to Closed. "Come back at six, Mister Cutter. The suit will be ready."

I needed a shave, so while Sol Gabriel got my suit in shape, I went hunting for a barber.

I spotted a striped pole over a stairwell leading to a basement shop. The sign over it read, "Louis Broglio Barber Service." As I went down the stairs, I could see through the window that the shop was brightly lit and two barbers were busy cutting hair.

Lou Broglio's shop was a compact space that looked bigger than it really was because of the mirrors that lined one wall, fronted by shelves stocked with bottles of hair tonic, Bay Rum, pomades, and other men's hair products. Two barber chairs and a little fire engine on a pedestal for kids.

A row of chairs lined one wall under coat hooks filled with overcoats and work jackets. The waiting customers included a businessman in a suit reading a newspaper, an old gent with a thick shock of white hair, and a burly guy in a work shirt reading one of the magazines from a rack beside the chairs. A radio in the corner was playing quiet music.

The barbers looked to be about sixty and thirty, respectively, and their faces looked stamped from the same die—father and son.

The door opened, and a man in a raincoat strolled in and said, "Hey, Lou. Hey, Junior," confirming my hunch. Instead of taking off his coat and sitting down, he walked across the shop and reached into the fire engine. He pulled out a paper sack with something squared off in it. He disappeared through the door and back to the street without another word.

Neither of the barbers blinked, and neither did the customers. Lou and Son were fronting a numbers operation, but so were a dozen other businesses in Washington, and for that matter every town up and down the Mon River Valley.

Lou took the cape off his customer, and the guy got out of the chair. Lou brushed him off and snapped the cloth, shucking the cut hair onto the floor, then he crooked a finger to the old man.

I had already seen the papers, so I pulled a week-old copy of *Life Magazine* out of the rack. I stared at the cover for a long time. It featured a picture of Raymond Massey made up as a convincing Abraham Lincoln for a Broadway show. Another guy wearing somebody else's face. The difference was that he was getting paid for it. Maybe someday, I thought, I could try Hollywood, if I lived through this little passion play.

A few pages later I saw pictures from the Empire Exhibition in Glasgow, Scotland beside preparations for the '39 World's Fair in New York. That's the good old U.S.A., I thought. Can't even pat somebody else on the back without showing them we'd do better.

The next few pages had a photo spread of a wolf hunt in Texas. I looked at the pictures of the hunters and their prey, and I felt like rooting for the wolves. I knew exactly how they felt. I closed the magazine and put back in the rack.

My turn came, and I drew the father. Lou waved me into the chair. It was an old one, lots of red leather and brass, exactly like the newer one Junior was tending, just more broken in.

"What'll it be, my friend?" The accent was slight, but definitely Italian.

"Trim and a shave."

I settled back in the chair and he laid the cape over me and buttoned the collar around my neck.

"You from town? Never seen you before."

"Passing through." To his credit, he took my terse answer as intended and didn't ask any more questions. He grunted and wet a metal comb in the sink behind me and slicked down my hair. He picked up a pair of long, thin shears with his other hand and went to work lifting my hair with the comb and snipping it with quick, bird-like moves.

Beside us, Junior was buzzing away with electric clippers.

"You always cut hair by hand? I mean, with scissors?"

"Yes, sir," Lou said proudly. "This is how I learned forty years ago , and this is how I'll cut hair 'til I die. Junior, he likes the change; me, I like the old ways."

The old ways were pretty good. I could see in the mirror that he was doing a fine job with my unruly hair.

"I was taught to cut every hair on a man's head the same length all over, and then it can lie naturally. You can't do that with the buzz, buzz, buzz. I'm not shearing sheep here."

I laughed in spite of myself at Lou's seriousness.

"Now the shave." He stepped on a lever and tilted the chair almost horizontal. He took a hot towel from the steamer behind him. The towel felt terrific. The muscles in my face were aching from hanging onto Mason's looks all this time. I could hear Lou stropping his razor. The radio was playing Glenn Miller's "Moonlight Serenade" and by the time it wound its way around the bridge, a day and a half's worth of running caught up with me.

A sharp pain jolted me awake.

"Holy Moses, I'm sorry, Mister." Lou was standing over me with the razor. I put my fingers to my cheek, and they came away bloody. "Your face twitched, kinda like you were having a spasm or something." He dabbed at my face with a styptic pencil. The alum stung as much as the cut.

"I dozed off, I guess I was dreaming. Not your fault." But I knew what it meant. My face was slipping. The longer I held Mason's face—or anybody's—the more conscious effort it took to keep it in place. I figured I was lucky my mug didn't snap back like a rubber band. That could have startled Lou enough for the razor to cut my throat.

Lou finished up, and when I paid him, he apologized again. "No worries," I told him.

I still had time on the clock before Sol would have my suit ready, so I figured it was a good time to call Mason. I found a phone booth in a drug store up the street from Lou's shop. It was just too damn cold for a long conversation at an outdoor phone. I bought a pack of Luckies and got some change for the phone.

The operator put me through to the office. The phone rang and rang; ten, twenty times, no answer. I waited fifteen minutes and called the designated booth on the hour. Mason answered on the second ring. "It's about goddamn time."

"Glad to hear your voice, too."

"This is round three for me. I've been hovering around this booth for hours. The phone company's gonna start charging me rent. Anyway, I got some news."

"Good, I hope."

"Good enough." Kobylarz and Watts were murdered with a .32, not your .38 or Kobylarz's service revolver. Not absolution, but heading that direction."

I fingered the badges in my pocket. "You know. I still have their buzzers. Maybe I oughta dump them."

"Don't do that. It makes sense that you'd keep them as proof they rousted you. You'd have to be nuts to keep them as souvenirs of a kill. Besides, anybody downtown who doesn't know that pair was dirty must be new on the job."

"I need you to do something for me, Mason. Send a couple hundred bucks to Mary Smith, registered at the Ritz-Carlton."

"Will do." There was a pause. "How's 'Mary' holding up?"

"She's next on my call list." I told him about the break-in and how I handled LaSorda and Vanner. "That pair sure as hell wasn't collecting for Catholic Charities that time of night. They figured to get to me through her. I want her on ice 'til this is over."

"Good plan."

"Maybe you could tap into some of your sources and find out what was up with the Bobbsey Twins."

"Info is expensive. It already cost me two fifths of Seven Crown to find out about the bullets."

"I'm good for it." I thought it over before I said, "You'll probably read about a certain Diamond Street pawnbroker in the papers."

"I heard it was a robbery but it looked hinky because there was a pile of jewelry in the open safe. Only thing missing was the cash. I heard Gus got a shot off."

"He took first turn. Nicked my ear."

"Humph. Sounds righteous. So, is there some way I can call you if I need to?"

"Sure. I'm at the George Washington Hotel."

"In Washington?"

"Is there another?"

"Only about five hundred from here to Frisco."

"I'm registered as Mason Cutter."

He snorted. "Don't steal the towels, they'll send the FBI after me and I could lose my license."

"More work for me."

Mason laughed and clicked off. It was a little after five, so I walked up Main Street to check on my suit. The sign was turned back to Open. I stepped inside and Sol came out of the back in shirtsleeves with the suit over his arm.

"It's done, Mister Cutter. Try it on."

I was impressed. The jacket hung on me like it was on a show window mannequin, even over my holster. I suspected that Sol had made the same accommodation more than once. The trouser cuffs broke just right over the vamp of my wingtips.

Looking in the mirror, I realized that my shirt was past redemption. I'd need a tie, too. By the time it was all wrapped up, I had the suit, three shirts, two ties, some socks and underwear, and a new pair of galoshes. My shoes needed a shine, but that I could get at the hotel.

Taking the weather into account, I bought a raincoat, since my waist-length jacket wouldn't cover the suit. My beat-up hat didn't belong with the new coat, so I sprung for a nicer grey fedora. I paid Sol with two C-notes and told him to keep the change. He stuffed my old duds in a sack, and I headed back to the GW.

Robert was still on duty when I came in the lobby. It was a little bit busier now. A dozen or so people were camped in the armchairs and sofas, reading newspapers, smoking cigars, and drinking highballs brought on a tray by a liveried waiter from the bar while they waited for their reservation times in the dining room.

Robert had his back to me, poking things into the numbered pigeon holes.

"Any messages for me? Three-seventeen. Cutter."

"No," he said brusquely. "There's nothing for—" He broke off his sentence when he saw me. The suit, the haircut, and the shave made an impact. "Uh," he stammered, "no messages."

I winked, shot him with a finger, and headed for the elevator. Instead of pushing my luck with Mason's face, I decided to have Room Service send up my supper. Steak, potatoes, green beans, and apple pie for dessert. And two bottles of beer; after all, Gus was buying.

Albert brought it up. He rolled my dinner in on a cart with a linen cloth that draped almost to the wheels and a silver dome over the tray.

He uncovered dinner. "There you are, Mister Cutter."

"Mason, Albert."

He nodded. "Mason. Right. Anything else I can do for you?"

"Not yet. How long are you on duty?"

"Ten o'clock."

"If I need anything else, I'll ask for you." I pressed a five into his palm, and to his credit, he didn't look at it. He slipped it into his pocket, smiled, and said, "Thanks—Mason." Albert stopped on his way out the door. "You know, Henry Ford stayed here once." He paused for effect. "And Al Capone."

"But not George Washington."

He laughed. "Nope, this is probably the one place in this end of Pennsylvania where he didn't stay."

"Henry Ford and Al Capone, huh? Then I guess I'm in good company."

He left, and my face came back. I don't think I ever ate a better meal.

It was time to call Marge. I figured by now she should be checked into her room.

The hotel phone, sitting on the writing desk was a Stromberg-Carlson Fatboy, mouthpiece and earpiece in the same handset. Nothing but the most modern features for the George Washington Hotel.

The GW's operator dickered with the Ritz-Carlton's operator and finally, I heard the ring on the other end in Mary Smith's room. It rang eight times, and I was about to hang up when Marge picked up.

"Hello?" She was out of breath.

"I was ready to give up on you, babe," I said with a laugh.

"You got me out of the bathtub," she growled. "Where are you?"

"Washington."

"I guess that's not too far. How'd you get there?"

"Don't ask."

"I was hoping you'd show up dressed in a bell hop uniform or some other stunt."

"Not yet, though the thought did cross my mind." Neither of us spoke for a minute. "So, what did you find out about McNairy?"

"Ready to write? There's a lot."

The secretary in my room had hotel stationery in the drawer. I skipped the pen and ink and opted for a pencil instead. I wasn't writing the Declaration of Independence, after all.

"I'll start with his pedigree. McNairy's a Fayette County boy. Third generation Grandfather Liam McNairy emigrated here from County Cork in the 70s. Father Michael McNairy, born in '78. Grew up to run his daddy's moonshine in a hopped-up car. The Revenuers chasing him ran him off the road into a stand of trees and he kinda got stuck halfway through the windshield.

"The irony is, he didn't have to die. When the agents approached the car, he started shooting at them. He killed one agent and hit two others before the whiskey in the car caught fire. The agents said, 'what the hell,' and let him barbecue.

"So, the apple landed right under the tree."

"No kidding. Francis was just a kid when his old man was killed. His mother ran off soon after, and he went to live with Grandpa Liam."

"Did he go into the family business too?"

"No, Liam sent Francis to a boarding school run by Jesuits."

"You're kidding."

"I guess Liam wanted to make sure the boy didn't end up like his old man."

"So much for good intentions."

"Francis Xavier McNairy went into racketeering early. His arrest record goes back to the tender age of eighteen, running numbers for the Republic operation. No conviction. As we both know, if the D.A. doesn't bring charges, it never goes to court."

Republic was a hub for Pennsylvania's underworld activity rivaled only by "little Chicago," New Kensington.

Marge went on. "He graduated to gambling, bootlegging, and extortion in the 20s. He ran a few scams on the side, small time stuff the Mob tolerated so long as it didn't interfere with their operations and they got their cut. But Irish Frank finally got nailed when he tried to blackmail a judge who was bopping his secretary. Frank got three to five for that one and got out after two years on good behavior.

"He was suspected of a few lowball heists, but the cops could never make them stick. Seems he cooked up some clever plots and managed to slip the noose."

"Looks like he made the most of his Jesuit education."

"He owns a house in South Hills and he was keeping a suite in the Livengood Arms."

"Livin' good in the Livengood. Who says crime doesn't pay?"

"The reports say the cops searched both places after the Diamond Exchange caper and found *bupkis*. No diamonds."

"And no getaway car."

"And no getaway car. And McNairy's on the early side of ten to twenty in the State Pen." I heard her shuffling papers, and realized I'd heard the end of her research. "So, what now, Mars? I don't have a bottomless purse."

"Mason's going to send some cash to you so you can stay put a little longer. I can keep myself out of harm's way, but I can't guarantee the same for you if I'm not there. And I can't concentrate on clearing myself if I have to worry about keeping your seams straight at the same time."

"What about work?"

"Call in sick. Think of it as a vacation."

"When this is over, Mars, if you're still walking and talking, I want a real vacation. You know what, Mars? I've never seen the ocean."

"Me either, Marge. When this is over, maybe we can go on a cruise."

"It's a date. And don't try to welsh on me and get yourself killed to get you out of it."

"You know me, babe. Don't worry."

"I do know you, Mars. That's why I do worry."

When we hung up, I never felt so alone in my life.

XIV

The telephone rang around nine o'clock. The switchboard operator said, "Mister Cutter, you have a collect call from a Mister Mars. Will you accept the charges?"

It was just like Mason to use my name as an alias. Oh well, turnabout and all that. "Yeah, put him through, please."

Mason's voice: "Mister Cutter?"

"Mister Mars," I said with a little more sarcasm than I intended.

"News for you. Big shootout in Bebe's Bar on Carson Street."

"I'm familiar with the place."

"Somebody went for Teddy Two-Tone. Two somebodies, actually. Teddy's sitting at the bar and these two hitters come in, make right for him with their hands in their coats. Long about then, Sal the bartender pulls a sawed-off .12 gauge from under the bar and a couple of hired hands slide out of a booth with their guns out.

"Teddy sits at the bar with his back to them, sipping his highball. Everybody else in the place just sorta freezes until Teddy finishes his drink. He turns real slow on the stool, rattling the ice in his glass, like he's shaking dice at a craps table.

"'You two looking for me?'" he says. Nobody says anything. 'Here's how it goes. Take your pieces out two fingers on the butt. Real slow.'

"The taller one cooperates, but his partner shouts, 'Nuts!' and pulls a .45. Before he can pull the trigger, Sal blows him in two with the sawed-off. The tall guy doesn't catch too much buckshot, but enough to put him on the floor. He damn near bleeds to death by the time the ambulance arrives.

"Teddy just sits there on his stool, cool as can be, looks at the bodies on the floor, shrugs, turns back to Sal, holds out his glass, and tells him, 'Hit me again,' Then he hands Sal a card and says, 'And then call this number.' The cops come and go, the ambulance comes and goes, and Two-Tone's still sitting on the stool."

"Who were the hitters?"

"Teddy's or the other guys?"

"Maybe I shoulda said the 'shootees,' not the 'shooters'. The other guys, you dope."

"Patsy Donohoe— he got whacked—and Marty Gallagher. Do the names suggest anything to you?"

"*Compadres* of Irish Frank."

"I'm betting."

"Where'd they take Gallagher?"

"Allegheny General."

"Maybe I'll pay him a visit."

"There's a uniform outside his door around the clock."

"I'll figure out something. He has to know a few things I don't that'll help clear me."

"Your funeral."

"Sooner or later, we all get one."

I desperately wanted to call Marge, to hear her voice and reassure

Sal the bartender pulls a sawed-off .12 gauge from under the bar...

myself that she was okay, but even more, I needed to remind myself that I had a reason to see this whole thing through and come out the other side. Okay, I'm a sap, but that also means that I'm human.

XV

Believe it or not, I slept pretty well. The outside world looked grey through the curtains, but at least the rain had stopped.

My face hurt like my biceps did when I'd do a workout after a long lay-off. I'd have to be careful about using my talent too often or too long. The barber shop incident was a warning shot.

I called Room Service to order breakfast: ham and eggs with home fries and coffee. The Room Service menu offered things like Crepes Bonaparte and avocado slices, but my appetite was one hundred percent American. I laid a buck on the secretary for a tip, and when the bellhop brought the cart, I told him to come in. Then I stepped into the bathroom while he brought in the food so he couldn't see my face.

"There's a buck for you on the desk," I called out through the door.

"Thank you, sir."

It wasn't Albert, but I didn't expect that it would be. He'd be off duty now, but I decided to leave him a tip at the desk for his service.

While I ate, I thought about my options. Pittsburgh was pretty hot for me, but I had to take a shot at bracing Marty Gallagher. I was convinced that it was Gallagher and Donohoe I shot it out with on Carson Street the night this whole caper began.

I decided to mail Jeffers one of the photo booth pictures. I wouldn't be back to Washington any time soon, so it didn't matter if he saw the postmark. I was tempted to mail it to him in a hotel stationery envelope, but that was an inch too far. I must admit, though, that the thought of a gang of coppers busting into the George Washington lobby and putting Robert under the hot lights did have its own appeal.

The suit surprised me all over again—how well it fit—when I checked myself out in the mirror on the back of the bathroom door. I packed my old duds and the extra clothes into the suitcase. One last detail: I concentrated on Mason's face. It hurt, a dull ache, as the muscles rearranged my features. This was the most I'd ever used a specific face, and you would think it would get easier, but it didn't.

It was a little after ten when I rode the elevator downstairs. I took the suitcase to the desk. Robert was on duty again, or maybe still for all I knew. I set the suitcase on the counter, its battered look contrasting sharply with the polished oak.

"Are you checking out, Mister Cutter?" I didn't think it was possible to sound snippy and hopeful at the same time, but he managed.

"Shortly. I have a few things to do first. Would you put my bag in the holding area for me?"

"Certainly." he reached for the suitcase.

"And could you give me two envelopes and a stamp? Plain envelopes, if you don't mind. You can put it on my bill."

He handed them over and took the bag. I slid a ten-dollar bill, wrapped in a sheet of hotel stationery so that nosy couldn't see what it was, into the envelope, sealed it, and wrote "Albert" on its face with the register pen. I was addressing the second envelope to District Attorney Ambrose Jeffers, care of the Allegheny Court House when Robert came back to the desk.

He did a poor job of trying to look as if he weren't trying to read the address upside down. I was writing left handed instead of my usual right, so I put my right forearm on the counter to shield the envelope. As an afterthought, I wrote the word "personal" in the lower left corner.

When I finished, I was about to put the stamp on the envelope when Robert said, "Would you like me to mail that for you, mister Cutter?"

I shook my head. "Not necessary. But you could lick the stamp if you like."

Robert sniffed and stalked off stage left. I licked the stamp myself and put the unsealed envelope in my pocket.

The hotel barber shaved me, this time without incident, probably because I was wide awake the whole time. The bootblack made my wingtips shine like new again, and I was ready to roll.

At the desk, I retrieved my suitcase and saw that the tiny spitballs I put under the buckles were still there. Apparently Robert's curiosity didn't get the best of him after all. If he'd have opened the bag, he would have found a note on top of my clothes that read, "nothing to see here, asshole."

I paid my tab with a hundred-dollar bill, just to force him to clean out his cash drawer early. I asked him for a receipt.

"Have my car sent around—Bobby." The bellhop snickered. Robert glared at him and picked up the phone to ring for the garage.

The tall grandfather clock in the lobby began the Big Ben carol. "How about that? Just under the wire." I stepped onto the sidewalk at the last stroke of eleven, the bellhop in tow with my bag.

The Packard gleamed. All the road grit from the day before had been washed off. I tipped the garage attendant and the bellhop five bucks each, sure that they would tell Robert what a generous guy I was and ask him what he got.

In the car, I tore off one of the photo booth snapshots of the key and the watch and slipped it into the stamped envelope. I sealed it, put the car in gear, and drove away from the GW in search of a post office.

On Wheeling Street, I found a snorkel box on the sidewalk right beside the hallowed wrought iron gates of Washington and Jefferson College, Jeffers' *alma mater*. Good enough; the picture was officially on its way to him. I wished that I could see his face when he opened the envelope

I was at a crossroads, literally. I could run the risk of driving back to Pittsburgh to try to talk to Gallagher, or I could take Route 40 to the next county to try to get a line on McNairy.

Mason didn't know exactly what shape Gallagher was in, so I figured I'd better go to the 'Burgh first. And yeah, I confess, I wanted to see Marge.

I aimed the Packard back up 19, the way I had come. The longer I drove the bad guys' car, the more I liked it. Too bad I couldn't keep it.

The sun shone through the overcast like a cold white eye. It was definitely November. The car's heater was running full blast, and it barely took off the chill. My Western Pennsylvania weather sense told me I'd see snow before sundown.

I switched on the radio and dialed through the static to KDKA. The station was playing recorded music, a selection of big bands. Guy Lombardo and his Royal Canadians were sashaying through their version of "Sentimental Journey". A few tunes later, the News at Noon came on with Uncle Ed Shaugnessey at the microphone. The guy's delivery was so jolly he could make a train wreck sound like a Harold Lloyd comedy.

The Pittsburgh City Attorney's case was heating up. Two as yet unnamed attorneys under indictment cutting deals with the D.A. That was funny. A crooked D.A., Jeffers, making deals with crooked lawyers—a professional courtesy. The cops were looking for three hoods who kidnapped a sixteen-year-old kid and stole his family's car, dropping the kid off later unharmed. Jacob Mintz, a local fight promoter got banged up in a car crash in Weirton, West Virginia. Japan suffered an earthquake.

Bottom line: I was no longer news.

I was relieved, but at the same time I couldn't let myself relax too much. The Pittsburgh P.D., on orders to shoot first and cuff me later, would still have its eyes out for me, and there were a hundred snitches who knew me on sight and would give me up for ten bucks and a cup of coffee. For that matter, there were at least that many people in the city who hated my guts and would do it for free.

I let my face slip into its normal look for the drive. I would have flipped down the sun visor, but on a day like today, it would look odd, and my freedom was riding on normal.

The ride into Pittsburgh was uneventful. By one-thirty, I was past Dormont and rolling down the long hill to the Liberty Tunnels. Coming out the city end of Mount Washington gives me the feeling that I lost a few hours going through the "Tubes." The mill smoke is so dense sometimes that it looks like twilight in the middle of the afternoon.

Allegheny General Hospital sits across the river on North Avenue. I circled the block a few times until I found a metered space. I didn't park in the hospital garage in case I had to make a quick exit.

I shifted my face just a little, enough, I hoped, to get past anyone who might otherwise recognize me from the papers. My face was sore, and I didn't want to push it too hard.

On the third floor, I saw the cop outside Gallagher's room. He was in uniform, Sam Browne belt and all. His name was Collins, an old war horse of a beat cop who never drew his pistol because he liked his nightstick better. He was propped against the wall in a chair, his big red potato of a nose stuck in a newspaper. I sat in the visitor's area down the hall where I could see Collins and the door, and watched for a while.

Being a successful private eye takes a lot of different traits, but I guess the biggest one, even over toughness and courage, is patience. Sometimes you just have to drop your hook in the water and wait for the fish to come to you.

An orderly in whites walked past the cop and nodded to him. He was familiar to Collins, who got out of his chair and unlocked the door. The orderly came back out in a few minutes with a tray. Collins locked the door again, and the orderly strolled down the hall. There was my ticket into Gallagher's room.

I stubbed out my cigarette and followed him at a discreet distance, watching his walk and his mannerisms. After a year or so of face-shifting, I figured out that the face wasn't always enough to be convincing. I noted how the orderly moved his arms, and held his head. His hair was just a wee bit lighter than mine, but I could get away without a hat. He passed a nurse's station and one of the Nightingales said, "Hi, Duane." He answered with a two-finger wave.

Duane turned a corner at the end of the hall and stepped into a room tagged "storage." He was lighting up a smoke when I came through the door.

"Hey, pal, you can't come in here. Staff only."

"Health Inspector." I flashed one of the cop badges too quick for him to read the fine print.

He took a drag on his cigarette and blew the smoke in my general direction. "So, what are you inspecting in here?" He was a wise-ass, and didn't care who knew it. I looked closely at his forehead, studying the stitch scar like the lacing of a tiny football just over his eyebrow.

"I'm inspecting disorderly orderlies, Duane."

He opened his mouth to shoot me another snappy comeback, and I shut it for him with an uppercut that knocked him backward into a rack of shelves. His eyes rolled up, and I caught him as he fell.

In five minutes, I was carrying an armload of bed linens down the hall, wearing Duane's whites—and his face.

I walked by Collins and he looked up from his paper. "What are you doing back here?"

I held up the linens. "Our special guest soiled his sheets. You have to open up so I can go in and change the bed. Of course, if you want, you can do it yourself."

Collins swore under his breath and heaved his bulk out of the chair. He unlocked the door, and I went in, giving him the two-finger wave on the way. He shut the door behind me, and I heard the click of the lock. I realized that I'd have to play this one carefully if I wanted to get out of here without handcuffs.

Speaking of which, a pair had Gallagher's right wrist shackled to the bed frame. He was asleep, snoring softly, so I clamped one of my mitts over his mouth and pinched his earlobe between the index finger and thumbnail of the other.

His eyes popped open, and he would have howled if he could. He tried to bite my fingers, so I let go of his ear and pinched his nostrils shut. He was weak but he still thrashed around, rattling the cuffs against the bed frame. I leaned close and said in his ear, "You want to breathe again, be still." After a few more tries, he settled down.

I took my hand off his nose. After a couple of panic gasps, his breathing slowed.

I pulled the switchblade from my pocket and held it where he could see me push the button and watch the blade swivel out of the blue pearl handle. I put the tip of the blade into the corner of Gallagher's eye.

"I'm going to take my hand off your mouth. If you talk to me, answer a few questions, everything will be fine. If you shout or piss me off, you'll be selling pencils for the rest of your life. Get me?"

He couldn't nod, but I could see by the look in his eyes that he knew the score. I took my hand from his mouth, and Gallagher was savvy enough to behave himself. With my free hand, I held the key in front of his face, and his eyes got wide.

"You recognize this, huh?"

Gallagher didn't speak, and he didn't move, but my cop eyes could see the gears turning between his ears.

"Tell, me, Marty, what's it for?"

He didn't answer right away, so I pushed a little with the tip of the knife. He got the message.

"Car." His voice was a dry-mouth whisper.

"What car?" I almost said McNairy's Hudson, but I didn't want him telling me what he thought I wanted to hear.

"Hudson."

"Whose car?"

"You know, smart guy, or you wouldn't be here."

I poked a little harder with the stiletto. "Whose car?"

"McNairy's Hudson."

"Now we're getting somewhere. Where is it?"

"Don't know."

"Why not? You were in on the diamond heist."

"Yeah, I was, but we split up right after, and Frank took the swag bag with him. We were going to meet up later, but he got nabbed."

"We being—"

"Donohoe and me, and the kid."

"The kid?"

"McNairy's wheel man. Never saw him before. Frank just called him Rusty. Patsy and I never knew his real name. Hell of a driver, though."

"So, you wanted this," I held up the key, "and you and Donohoe killed Billy Cramer for it."

He didn't answer. Instead, he heaved a sigh and said, "All those jobs we did with Frank. They all went off like clockwork. His plans were great, but the take was always chicken feed. Then the one time we could make a big score—"

I heard the click of the key in the lock. Collins was coming in. I thought fast and cold cocked Gallagher. By the time Collins got the door open, I was pulling the sheet up to Gallagher's chin.

"Thanks, officer." I hustled out of the room and didn't look back. I kept waiting for the Long Arm of the Collins to snag me by the shirt collar, but it never happened. I got to the supply room and found Duane, still out cold, trussed hand and foot with adhesive tape, just like I left him.

I switched duds, put on my hat and coat, and walked out wearing Walter Winchell's face under my hat brim.

Everything kept coming back to the car. Irish Frank's Hudson was at the core of the case. I wondered if the black and silver Terraplane was a special order or he bought it off the lot. To find that out, I couldn't do another B and E. Assuming the watchman found the unlocked door of the dealership a few nights ago, I'd figure he was running his rounds more closely. I could have kicked myself for not just lifting the file with the sale papers. I was already on the right side of the river. Why not find out now. I fingered the badges in my pocket. Eenie, Meenie, Miney . . .

I walked into Warner Motors wearing Watts's shield on my lapel and Czap's face. Charles Warner, the owner of the dealership was irritated at the intrusion, but when I raised my voice and said a few things about police business in his showroom where some rich folks were eyeing up his stock, he took me to his office.

"The case is closed, and Mister McNairy is in prison." Warner said, sitting behind his mahogany barricade of a desk, arms folded, the picture of indignation. "Why are you bothering me about it now?"

"The Department is looking into the case again," I lied.

"We sold Mr. McNairy a car. He used it in a robbery. We're no more responsible for that than the dealer who sells you your pistol is, if you use it to shoot someone."

"Was the car a special order? Anything unusual about it?"

"Not a thing. It came right off the floor. "

"May I see the file?"

"I gave the police a photostatic copy. What happened to that?"

"It's missing in action. Will you give me the file, or do I go back out on the floor and tell Mister Plushbottom and his Missus what a cooperative, upstanding citizen you aren't."

Warner snorted and swiveled his chair to the filing cabinet. He started to open the second drawer, and I almost said, "No, not that drawer, the next one," but I caught myself in time.

He finally opened the right drawer and pulled out the file. "Here it is."

I flipped the folder open. Everything was standard procedure. Tax and title paid, registered with the Bureau of Motor Vehicles, the works. I almost missed a small handwritten note at the bottom of the page. The bottom line was half missing because the carbon paper was out of line: an address.

"This address is different from McNairy's residence."

Warner squinted at it. "Oh, I remember now. He asked us to deliver the car, so we did. "

"I don't recall seeing this in the report."

"Well, apparently the officer who came here right after the robbery didn't notice."

Part of the address was missing, but I didn't need it. I recognized the rest. The address belonged to Canonsburg Auto Repair, Art McCurdy's body shop. Art had some explaining to do.

Next stop, the Ritz-Carlton.

I drove over the Sixth Street Bridge back into Downtown. The sun kept trying, I'll give it that, but it never quite broke through the special mix of cloud and coal smoke that lay over Pittsburgh like a shroud.

On Fifth Avenue, the afternoon traffic was heavy. I was waiting out a red light when a trolley rattled by, its contact antenna throwing sparks off the overhead cable. Just like life passing McNairy by, I thought.

So Irish Frank was some kind of criminal mastermind, a little dog on a narrow tether who wanted to be a big one. I could understand McNairy's frustration with his Eye-tie bosses, holding him down because he was a Mick, giving the big stuff, the plum jobs to their sons and nephews while Frank believed he was destined for greater things than a candy store stickup. He'd run a terrific plan, and the bosses would yawn. No matter where you sit on the bank, there's always somebody upstream pissing in the river.

Given a free hand, Irish Frank may have become a Moriarty to Agronski's Inspector Lestrade. Naah, that's stretching it. But he was smart enough to plan the diamond heist and get away with it, at least in the short run. All he had to do was wait. The diamonds would be waiting, and only he knew where they were.

Did McNairy cut a deal with Jeffers for a bite of the loot? If he did, it was a lousy one; ten to twenty years lousy. I could imagine that snake Jeffers telling Frank he'd get off with a light sentence, or maybe Jeffers would throw the fight, lose the case on some stupid technicality and let McNairy walk.

So, McNairy tells Jeffers about the Hudson, but hedging his bets, Frank the Genius gives Jeffers a fake location on the car. In the meantime, Jeffers swipes the key out of evidence, double-crosses Frank and throws the book at him. Frank gets ten-plus, and Jeffers has been looking for the Hudson ever since.

I was sure Jeffers didn't find it, otherwise, he wouldn't be keeping the key in a lockbox with the family jewels. I was convinced that Gus Legatto knew a hell of a lot more than I got out of him before I had to shoot him. I figured Gus had inside info about the jewel shipments and conned Frank into thinking he would steal ten grand worth of diamonds, Gus would fence them for a hundred and pocket the difference. If McNairy squawked, Gus would tell him the Diamond Exchange exaggerated the take for the insurance company.

Gus knew what the key was all about the minute Billy Cramer showed it to him, but he must have thought he died and went to Hoodlum Heaven when he saw the watch in the same bag and realized he had the D.A. on a big, sharp hook. If he knew about the key, he likely knew that Donohoe and Gallagher were McNairy's hired help, and he opened the bidding.

A horn blared behind me. The light was green, and my head was off someplace else. I rolled up Fifth working my way through the traffic toward the William Penn. At one intersection I passed within three feet of Wally Byers, someone from my class at the Academy, directing traffic, waving his arms like a crazy conductor and blowing his whistle every other breath. He looked right at me through the windshield but didn't blink. Too busy exercising his authority to notice a wanted man, I suppose.

I pulled to the curb in front of the William Penn, and the uniformed attendant ran around to open the door for my neighbor Ralph's face on my body.

"Get my bag, would you please." I handed the keys to the attendant. He whistled for the bellhop, and a tall guy in a long red coat with gold epaulettes and an admiral's hat on his head bowed and opened the door for me.

The George Washington was ritzy, but the William Penn was elegant, if you catch the distinction. It reeked of big money and old money, taste and class. If I had the concession to clean all the brass and glass in the lobby, I'd die rich. As I crossed to the desk, I could hear a piano playing. A guy in white tie and tails was playing something classical on a grand piano for whoever happened to be walking by at three in the afternoon. Fresh cut flowers—in November—rested in crystal vases on the tables for nobody in particular. It was as if the hotel existed for itself and nobody else. We mere humans were just more decoration.

I got a room. If this was some fleabag, I could have just waltzed onto the elevator, no suitcase, and ridden right up to Marge's room. But this was the William Penn Hotel, the largest hotel east of the Mississippi River. If I walked in off the street and tried to go to an unescorted lady's room, Artie Preston, the hotel dick would be on the phone to Vice, after a suitable amount of time with his eye to the keyhole, "researching" the situation.

I registered as Arthur Forbes of Omaha, Nebraska, and the desk clerk smiled, handed me the key to 832, and said, "Enjoy your stay, Mister Forbes. Please let us know if there is anything we can do to make it more pleasant." What a difference a suit makes.

The room was actually a suite, a sitting room and a bedroom with its own door to the hallway and a bath connected. The wall paper was a nice muted stripe pattern and the blue carpet was as thick as my grandfather's beard, but a lot softer. The furniture was first rate too, a pair of overstuffed chairs and a settee grouped around a coffee table, and a secretary to one side of the door. The whole thing was lit by clamshell wall fixtures that cast a soft glow around the room if you didn't want to use the brighter ceiling light.

The bellhop asked me if I needed any further services. I decided that maybe I should have my old clothes laundered in case I needed a change. He opened a drawer in the bedroom dresser and pulled out a canvas laundry sack. "If you like, sir, please put your things in this bag and set it outside the door. I'll pick it up shortly, and your clothes should be ready in the morning."

I tipped him and he left. I locked the door behind him and made a beeline for the phone. I got the operator on line and asked her to connect me with Mary Smith's room.

"One moment, please."

This time she answered on the first ring.

"Not in the tub this time, huh?"

"I've taken so many baths out of sheer boredom that I'm about waterlogged. Where are you?"

"I'm in room 832 of the William Penn Hotel. Where are you?"

"Room 419."

"I'll be right down."

"Wouldn't you rather I came up there? You might be seen."

"You might too, and I'm a professional sneak, remember. Hey, if you think about it, you might call Room Service and have them send up a bottle of bourbon and some ice."

"Sure thing."

"Like I said, I'll be right down."

I rode the elevator to the lobby then stood near the car until a group of people got on and said, "Four," to the operator. I stepped in as he was about to close the cage and rode up with a half dozen men in town for a doctor's conference of some kind. I melted into the gang as the car went up and the operator paid me no mind when we all got off. For safety's sake, I followed the crowd around the corner toward their rooms until the elevator door closed and the needle tipped to the lower floors.

I tapped on the door of 419 and I heard Marge say, "Who is it?"

"The Big Bad Wolf," I growled. "Let me in, or I'll huff and I'll puff—"

She opened the door. "You don't have to prove to me you're a blowhard. I—" Her eyes popped when she saw my face, and I remembered I still looked like Ralph.

"Sorry." I thought real hard, and my own face came back. I stepped into the room and closed the door behind me.

"I'll never get used to that, Mars. As long as I live, I'll never get used to that. Nice suit, by the way. That threw me more than your face."

I wrapped my arms around her and kissed her hard. It took a few seconds, and then she started kissing me back. When we came up for air, I said, "Glad to see you." Over her shoulder, I spotted a tray on the desk with a bottle of Old Grand Dad, two glasses and an ice bucket.

"Glad to see you too, Grand Dad." Keeping an arm around Marge, I walked her over to the desk. I uncorked the bottle and poured myself a good belt and drank it down neat. They've been making Old Grand Dad for almost a hundred years, and it took them almost that long to get it right, but once they did, there was no better label.

I poured another for myself and one for Marge. I dropped some ice cubes in both. "So, how do you like the leisure life?"

"I'd like it fine if it wasn't confined to two rooms and a bathtub. That and no change of clothes."

"Well, I'm hoping it won't be much longer before the heat's off, and then you can come and go as you please."

"I've taken so many baths out of sheer boredom that I'm about waterlogged."

"I'll go all right, but I won't be coming back here; not at these rates."

"Did Mason send you money?"

"Two hundred bucks."

I pulled out my roll and peeled off a couple of Gus's hundreds. "Put that with the rest."

"What'd you do, stick up a filling station?"

"You'd be surprised how much green they keep in the register."

"So, tell me, Mars, where are we in the stream of things?"

I gave her a run-down, leaving out a few of the gorier details, and when I was done, she just shook her head. "Why couldn't I fall for a nice boring accountant?"

"The same reason I couldn't fall for a nice boring librarian." I grinned. "We're two of a kind: both nuts."

She punched me on the arm. "So, do we call down for supper before or after?"

"Before or after what?" I teased, already knowing the answer.

"Before I take off your gun and drag you into the next room." I kissed her again, a little gentler this time and said, "You decide." On the way to the bedroom, I turned toward the door and waved to the keyhole, just in case Artie was watching. Eat your heart out, gumshoe.

Like my room upstairs, the bedroom had twin beds with chocolate-colored spreads and lace-trimmed pillows. In one corner I saw a lighted vanity table strewn with Marge's secret weapons: lipstick, face powder, rouge, mascara, brushes, combs, and perfume. The bathroom door was ajar, and I could see Marge's lingerie hanging to dry from the towel rack.

"Don't mess up the second bed," she said, falling back across the first one and posing like a Vargas calendar pin-up. "They'll think I snuck a friend in on the cheap."

She was right. No matter how carefully you made the second bed, the chambermaids always knew somebody slept in it.

"Kinda narrow for two people."

"Not if you stack them like cord wood. "

And that was the last thing either of us said for a while.

XVII

"**I** never figured out why people smoke after a roll in the hay," Marge said, watching the wisps drift between the bed and the ceiling.

"Don't ask me. You're the brains of this consortium." She was lying on her back, the sheet pulled up to her navel and the ashtray between her breasts. I was lying on my side ready to roll off onto the floor if I breathed the wrong way.

"That's a good word. Consortium." It sounded sexy, almost indecent the way it slid off her tongue.

"You taught it to me."

"I mean it's a good name for it. People consort, right, so two people consorting are a 'consortium.'"

"Yeah, I get it."

"But there's one hitch. The definition of consortium is, "the right of association and companionship with one's husband or wife."

Here it comes, I thought.

"Something to aim for, huh, Mars?"

I took a deep pull on my cigarette, something I often did to stall for time to think up an answer. I figure some of the world's greatest responses are delivered in a cloud of cigarette smoke.

"I hate to make promises I'm not sure I can keep. Let's work on the cruise first."

Marge sighed and stubbed her cigarette out in the ashtray. "And I'm the one with the brains?"

Neither of us said anything for a while. Finally, the mood gone, Marge rolled face-to-face and said, "So now what do we do, Mars? I can't stay in this room for the rest of my life and eat bon-bons and listen to the radio."

"If the wrong people find you, babe, you may spend the rest of your life in this room, as little of it as may be left."

"What are you going to do next?"

"Gallagher said something about a young kid, a wheel man for McNairy. Gallagher didn't know him, just his nickname, Rusty, which means he's imported talent. Who are the best getaway drivers in Pennsylvania?"

She thought about that one for a minute. "Moonshine runners."

"Right. And where's the moonshine capital of Pennsylvania?"

"Fayette County. I'm guessing the kid's from McNairy's old stomping grounds."

"Home of the Whiskey Rebellion."

"The what?"

"Did you sleep through grade school history class, Mars?"

It seems the moonshine business has its roots in a long-standing Pennsylvania tradition. The U.S. of A. wasn't twenty years old when a gang of citizens were ready to overthrow the new government over the taxing of liquor. Because it was cheaper and easier to transport a gallon of whiskey than it was to haul a couple of bushels of corn over the mountains, the farmers all ran stills and the whiskey became a second kind of money.

When the government enacted the so-called "liquor tax," it was the first internal income tax the country had ever seen, and the Pennsylvania farmers took it personally. So much so, that John Gaddis of Hopwood organized a rag-tag force and built a stockade on his farm. Tax collectors were routinely beaten, tarred, and feathered. At one point, a mob of five hundred men attacked the home of a federal tax collector and burned it to the ground. George Washington sent 13,000 troops to stop the rebels, and the farmers gave up the fight—overtly. And for the next hundred years or so the whiskey business was driven underground, to become a main staple of Fayette County's economy.

"So, you're going to Fayette County to look for this driver."

"It's a lead, babe. I figure it's better than hanging around this town waiting for some zealous cop to shoot me. And now that I've rattled Jeffers' cage, I expect things will get hotter."

"You didn't show your face in the picture, just the key and the watch. How could he know it's you?"

"He doesn't, for sure, but he knows it could be me, so he's keen to get me out of his shadow, just in case. I know enough to cause him a lot of grief, but I need enough to put him away for good."

"Take me with you."

"No way."

"Think about it, Mars. Nobody out there in the boonies knows who I am, but I'm betting your face made the papers even in Podunk. I'm no slouch at research, as we both know. I can dig through the Court House records in half the time it would take you, if you even knew what to look for. Plus, I'm an extra set of eyes to watch your back."

I thought about it for a minute and decided Marge was making sense. "Okay, you can come with me. But you have to do what I tell you if things get tight."

"No argument. You're in charge."

"Sometimes brains aren't a match for instinct."

Room Service brought me a steak and Marge almond-crusted salmon, and wine to wash it down. She said I needed red wine for my steak, and white wine for her fish, so we ordered a bottle each.

"You know, Mars, this is really living. Forget what I said about being confined."

"That's the wine talking, Marge. Tell me that again in the morning."

I went back to my room around midnight, not wanting to attract undue attention from Artie or any of the staff. It would be just my luck to have the Vice Squad bust in on me asleep with Marge like the mainliners did to McNairy and his coochie squeeze. Marge still had the pistol I gave her and she promised me she'd keep it under her pillow.

I had another reason to separate myself. I needed to see Mason, and I didn't want Marge tagging along, mostly for her own safety. I called his apartment from a phone booth in the hotel lobby and lucked out. He was at home.

"Yeah?"

"Guess who."

"Henny Youngman by the sense of humor."

"Did you hear the one about the private eye who—"

"Can it. Regular place?"

"Duck soup."

"Be on time, and wear your hat." He hung up.

The regular place was the Tavern on Market Square. "On time" meant on the next hour. "Wear your hat" meant don't wear one. Market Square was a short walk, so I didn't need to take the car. Not wearing a hat was a good idea and a bad one. It was a good one because it would throw the cops a curve ball in case they had a tap on the line and were listening in and tried to intercept me before Mason showed up. Also, since I wouldn't be wearing my own face, either, it was a way to spot me more easily. It was a bad idea because the temperature had dropped a good ten degrees since sundown, and the wind was blowing sleet.

The ear that Gus grazed with his pistol stung from the cold as I turned the collar of my raincoat up around my face. The sleet felt like needles. By the time I got to Market Square, I regretted leaving the Packard in the garage.

The Tavern still had a lively crowd, most of the tables full, and I had to walk two-thirds of the way around the oaken bar before I found an empty stool. I was glad to be out of the cold, but my ear switched from stinging to a dull, steady throb. There was a cure for that, though, and I ordered a double dose.

Mason came in five minutes later. He spotted me wearing his brother's face across the room. There wasn't an empty stool nearby, so he got a beer and we moved to a booth in the back near the nickelodeon—I guess they call them jukeboxes now— where we couldn't be easily overheard.

"News?"

"Some. Your pals LaSorda and Vanner were booked on drunk and disorderly charges. LaSorda made his one phone call, and in an hour, Uncle Benny bailed them out. Benito "Uncle Benny" Tassone was the unofficial bondsman for Pittsburgh's underworld.

The rumor was that he never slept for more than an hour at a time because his phone rang so often, but at ten o'clock at night or four in the morning, or five in the afternoon, the dapper little man showed up in a starched white shirt with a fresh shave and a carnation in his lapel. Everybody knew that Uncle Benny wasn't putting up his own money; he was just a front for the Mob, toting their cash to the police station. It was a rare case when one of the connected spent twenty-four hours in lockup for anything short of murder.

"We knew they were crooked anyway. So what?"

"So, they're let out on the street, go back to Algonquin, and guess what: LaSorda's car is missing."

"I'm shocked. What's this city coming to, when a pair of gunmen can't leave their car parked at three in the morning without it being stolen."

"You're racking up a big tally, Ike; assaulting two police officers, killing Legatto, stealing a car."

"Don't forget breaking and entering, impersonation —and creating a public nuisance."

"That last goes without saying."

"You left out turning the vise on Jeffers' nuts. Or is that a crime?"

"More like a public service." He drank some of his beer. "I also heard that McNairy is taking a vacation. Some fancy mouthpiece got him an appeal on the robbery, and he's going to court in a couple of days."

"Where?"

"Here. Judge Swetz is hearing the case. He's on the pad, so maybe Frank will walk."

"He's on the pad, and he's also under Jeffers' thumb."

"Question is, does Jeffers want him walking around?"

"I'm guessing no, but it sure seems funny that he'd get an appeal this week, doesn't it?"

"If I was Irish Frank, I'd make sure I had my will drawn up."

"But only after he spills the location of the car. I'm guessing once he's in the Allegheny County Jail, they'll beat it out of him."

"Then maybe Jeffers won't need the key. It's just a car. Maybe with a trick lock, but it's just a car."

"No, there's more to it. Has to be. Otherwise, people wouldn't be shooting each other to get their hands on the key."

Mason's eyes snapped up. He was looking at something over my shoulder. He mouthed the word "Czap."

"Out for a nightcap, Cutter?" Czap stood beside the booth, but neither Mason or I slid over to invite him to sit. Montrose stood behind Czap, his hand in his pocket as a subtle threat. "Haven't heard from your partner lately, have you?"

"I hope he comes back soon. Rent on the office is due next week and he owes half."

"Who's your buddy?"

"This is my cousin Al from Erie. Al Cutter, say hello to Pittsburgh's answer to Dick Tracy, George Czap, and his comical sidekick Mike Montrose." George smirked, but Montrose was stone-faced.

Czap looked me over pretty close. "I can see the family resemblance, especially the ape-like forehead and the nose." He pushed his lips out and blew a breath. "If I didn't know better, Cutter, I'd swear it was the ghost of your brother." Then he did something I didn't see coming. He grabbed my nose between his index and middle fingers. He gave it a quarter twist and let go. He laughed. "And it's real."

"You done, George?" Mason said with feigned irritation in his voice.

"For now." he turned to me and said, "If you haven't eaten yet, try the duck soup. I hear it's pretty good, unless, of course you find a fly in it." He turned to Mason. "If you do hear from Mars, you'll give me a jingle, won't you."

"Did it ever occur to you that maybe he didn't kill the Bobbsey Twins?"

Czap grinned. "Never for a moment. If he's innocent, why did he run?"

"Maybe so the hitter who killed Watts and Kobie can't do him the same turn."

"Your partner's a millstone, Cutter. Don't fall off a bridge." He grinned again, and he and Montrose strolled out the door without looking back.

"I figured they had a tap on my phone by now, but I didn't think any cop was good enough to tail me."

"Czap isn't just any cop. How long do you think it'll take for him to find out you don't have a cousin Al in Erie?"

"Not long enough. You planning to leave town any time soon?"

"With the sunrise."

"And Marge?"

"By my side."

"Good. Oh, by the way, a broad named Gloria Swenson called the office. She wanted to know whether you made any headway on her case. Guess she doesn't read the papers."

I slid two C-notes across the table, and with a move worthy of a magician, Mason snapped them up, folding them as he did, and they were gone. He left first. I gave it ten minutes and headed out myself. The wind had died down and the sleet had turned to snow, covering the gritty bricks for a while.

I strolled out of the square, certain that Montrose was behind me. There were enough people on the sidewalks that my footprints weren't the only ones to follow. At an intersection, I jumped a moving trolley headed across the river, and as I looked back, I saw Montrose under a street light, too far away to catch up with the car. I was glad Czap was tailing Mason and not me. Czap wouldn't have let that happen.

I rode the trolley to the North Side and as we passed through the Spanish War District and watched the Stearns and Foster warehouse and Warner Motors slide past the windows. I hopped off the trolley and lucked out, hailing a passing cab to take me to the William Penn.

Back in my room, I ran hot water onto a washcloth and held it against my aching ear. I opened my suitcase and found the half empty pint of bourbon Albert had brought me at the George Washington. It seemed like a month since I'd been there. I poured two fingers to kill the pain in my ear, and in five minutes, I was sawing logs, the chenille bedspread pulled up to my chin.

XVIII

The phone woke me. No matter how deeply I sleep, two things wake me up without fail, the sound of somebody turning the bedroom doorknob, and a ringing telephone. The sound hooked me by the ear and jerked me out of bed and across the sitting room like a trout before I was fully conscious.

"Mars, are you awake?" It was Marge.

"I am now."

"I'm ready to check out."

"What time is it?"

"Eight-thirty."

"Give me a few minutes." I normally woke before seven, but yesterday wore me out. The booze didn't help my cause, either. I was lucky the hotel didn't catch fire. I would have slept through the whole thing. I called Room Service to send up a pot of coffee.

I had my suit on by the time the coffee arrived, and by the time I tied my necktie a bellhop was at the door with my laundered clothes. I packed them into my suitcase and sat down to tie my shoes. The phone rang again. I didn't bother picking up. I knew it was Marge.

I took a last look at how the other half lives, threw my raincoat over my arm, grabbed my suitcase, and made for the elevator. I rode to the ground floor and was paying my bill when Marge came out of the elevator. I handed over the key. "Thank you, Mister Forbes." The clerk handed me my receipt. "Please come see us again."

It was getting to be a full-time job keeping all my aliases straight. I winked at Marge as I walked away from the counter. I stopped to light a cigarette, long enough to hear, "Shall we call you a taxi, Miss Smith?"

"No thank you. I've made other arrangements."

The garage sent the Packard around front, and I climbed in. I waited a minute, and Marge stepped past Admiral Doorman, who scurried to open the passenger door for her. Marge was wearing her good winter coat, the one with the fur collar, and a pill box hat. The Admiral put her suitcase in the back seat and we were off.

The sky was the patented Pittsburgh grey. Maybe an inch of snow lay on the unpaved ground, of which there wasn't much downtown. The streets and sidewalks were slush, and a few random flakes swirled in front of the windshield as we drove through the concrete canyons.

"What's the best way to Fayette County?" I asked her.

"You have two choices, Route 19 to Washington then 40 west, or Route 51 south. Both ways take you to Uniontown, the County Seat."

"Which way's better?"

"Never been either way. Flip a coin. And turn up the goddamned heater, will you?"

"Let's take 19. I have to see a man about a car."

I'd never been to Uniontown, but I was sure the city had a good women's clothing store to set Marge up with a few outfits, so when we came out of the Tubes, I shot up the hill and headed south on 19.

We decided to stop between Peters Township and Canonsburg for breakfast at a diner that wasn't busy at that hour of the morning. It was one of those pre-fab aluminum buildings designed to look like a train car with a long counter and a line of pedestal stools. I put on Ralph's face and took Marge in by the elbow. The diner was all but empty, so we took stools near the register.

I ordered the breakfast special, bacon, eggs, and toast. Marge settled for the toast. The waitress, a cute red head, stopped by to keep our coffee cups full, but she spent most of her time down the counter flirting with a young guy who was dressed as if he belonged to the delivery truck in the lot. He apparently belonged to more than that, based on the wedding ring on his finger, but he was giving as good as he got. Who knows? Maybe in six months or a year, I'd be trailing those two to some hot pillow joint for the wife. No doubt about it; human nature keeps me in groceries.

Marge buttered her toast and took dainty bites, chewing them to disintegration. I shoveled in the food like I was firing a blast furnace. I was on the last bite of bacon, and she was just buttering her second piece of toast.

"Forget what I said last night. I can't imagine waking up every morning and sitting across the breakfast table watching you eat. It's like staring into a cement mixer."

"Just as well," I said. "Imagine stationery with the name Marge Mars on it."

"It's unanimous." She took another bite of the toast. "But you still owe me the cruise."

"Fair enough." I lit a cigarette and sipped my third cup of coffee.

"When we get to Uniontown, I'll take the Court House records. You take the newspaper files. They should be in the library."

"What am I looking for?"

"Go back two years before the heist. Arrests for moonshine running. Any mention of McNairy. Get the names of drivers and suppliers. I'll go through court records first, and then once I have some names, I'll compare them with whatever you find. Maybe we'll find Rusty. If not, I can guarantee you one of us will find the name of at least one person who knows him. "

"Like I said about the brains."

"If I'm so damned smart, why am I still sitting here with you?"

"Just lucky, I guess. Me, not you."

"Glad you cleared that up."

We finished our coffee and got up. The waitress rang it up on the register, and I looked out the door just in time to see a guy in a moth-eaten sweater, a newsboy cap, and a bandanna over his face crossing the parking lot. He had a shiny chrome-plated revolver in his hand. "Oh, hell."

"What?" Marge looked around and said, "Oh."

Marge and I had our backs to him when the bandit yanked the door open and came in. "This is a stick-up. Turn around and put 'em up."

Marge and I turned around, and he found himself looking down two-gun barrels. Granted, mine was bigger, but that close, Marge couldn't miss, and he couldn't survive hers any better.

His eyes got wide. I could see four out of six chambers in the cylinder. No horses on the carousel. If he didn't have one under the hammer, he was out of ammo. Another victim of the Depression, I guess; had the cash for the gun but not for the bullets.

I cocked the .38. "You put 'em up. You're running on empty, bud."

The cook, a feisty little guy with a long apron and a grease hat came running out of the kitchen with a meat cleaver in his hand. At first, he thought we were the robbers, and started for me, and then he saw the guy's bandanna and wised up. I stepped back, gestured with an open palm, and told him, "He's all yours."

The would-be John Dillinger's eyes darted wildly. He let out a sound someplace between a scream and a moan, spun on his heel, and ran through the door. He tripped on the top step and fell face down in the parking lot gravel. He didn't even stand up; the poor sap scrambled on all fours around the front of the truck and took off running across the road. He disappeared into the trees. I looked down the counter and saw the truck driver huddled under his stool.

The waitress was about to hand me my change when the would-be robber first came in. She was still standing open-mouthed with two quarters and a dime in her hand. She blinked back into reality. "Uh, your change, Mister."

"Keep it."

It was all we could do to keep from busting out laughing until we got into the car, and once we did, it was like a dam broke. All the danger, the tension, the worry of the last couple days let loose, and we howled. I laughed so hard I damn near drove the Packard into a ditch. We'd wind down, get to breathing almost normally, and then we'd look at each other and start all over again.

The cook came running out of the kitchen with a meat cleaver in his hand.

"When this is over, Mars, I'm gonna write a book."

Maybe Hollywood'll make it into a movie. Who do you think would play my part?"

"That's a tough one. Karloff's too good looking, and Buster Keaton's too short."

"Thanks a lot, Marge. I was going to cast Olivia de Haviland in your role, but after that last crack, I'm going for Zazu Pitts. Or maybe I'll think of somebody even better."

"Give your brain a rest, Mars. You'll need it when we get to Uniontown."

I pulled up to McCurdy's garage and told Marge to wait in the car. I walked to the customer door. The Closed sign showed in the glass, but I could hear the air compressor running. I tried the knob, and the door swung open. "Art?" No answer. I walked through the office and back into the bay. A Cadillac sedan was on the lift, and Art was under it, the breath crushed out of him. His eyes were wide open, and a thin line of blood ran from the corner of his mouth to drip on the concrete. I looked to the lift control. I guess Art could have pulled the handle himself—if his arms were eight feet long. I imagined the killer letting the lift down a little at a time, squeezing answers out of Art then squeezing the last breath out him when he ran out of them.

I closed his eyes and left, wiping my prints off the doorknob as I shut the door.

I climbed in the car and didn't say anything for a minute.

"Well, what did you find out?"

"That we're dealing with a lot bigger bear than I ever saw in these woods."

XIX

There was almost no snow on the ground as we rolled past mile after mile of farmland and emptiness 'til we came to Route 51. The two-laner wound and twisted through hills and valleys, following the path of least resistance like flowing water. The few cars we saw were mostly headed in the opposite direction.

We passed more than one coke yard, the brick ovens belching out thick black smoke that smelled like Hell's back yard from the sulfur. For a while, the road ran alongside a wide creek that shone a muddy orange color in the pale sunlight.

"That's Redstone Creek," Marge said. "I read once that George Washington said that it had the best trout fishing in Pennsylvania."

"Yellow boy."

"Huh?"

"That's what my late uncle Randall called the yellow in the creeks from the mine drainage. It's mostly sulfur."

"I guess that's why they drink so much beer. Safer than the water."

"Beer and moonshine." I said, pointing through the windshield. "From up there."

Ahead, we could see the mountains, looking like somebody kicked up a white throw rug and left it rumpled in the hazy distance. The Allegheny Mountains lay like a barrier at the end of the world. Although I knew better, it gave me the feeling that once I got to the crest, I'd look over it and see nothing on the other side, as if it was my last stop on a long, tough road.

The last five miles into Uniontown took a lot longer than it should because we were following a hay wagon that left little room to pass on the narrow road. Going slowly gave us the time to take a good look at the area. We passed a couple of "patch" towns, small villages made up of a half dozen rows of clapboard two-family houses thrown up by the companies next to a mine or a coke yard. I saw thin wisps of smoke from some of the chimneys and none from others. It was a cold winter to be out of work and out of money.

We passed the spidery tower of a coal tipple almost abutting the road. Its huge spoked flywheels were idle in the grey morning, when they should have been pulling cars full of coal from the shaft. The Recovery either hadn't arrived here yet, or maybe it just stepped over Fayette County on its way to someplace else.

The wagon finally turned off, and in a few minutes, we rolled into the thriving metropolis. The first two things I saw at opposite ends of the town were the tallest buildings, a big ochre high-rise to the west, and the dark stone clock tower of the court house to the east. They stood at either end of the town's main street like a pair of bookends with little to hold between them. The buildings between were at the most, three stories tall and were dwarfed by the majestic ones.

The courthouse clock read eleven-fifteen. I used it as a guidepost to navigate my way through the tangle of streets and alleys that cross-hatched the town like scars from a knife fight. I parked on Main Street in front of the building. It looked like a castle from some storybook, but its once white limestone had been blackened by decades of soot, which made it look menacing in the dim light. An arch connected the Court House with the County Jail, both fashioned from the same limestone, and looking equally imposing. The Bridge of Sighs, people called the arch.

Marge grabbed her purse and reached for the door handle. "Here's where I get off. You go to the library and look through the newspapers."

"Where's the library?"

"You're the detective, Mars. Go find it." She stepped out onto the sidewalk. "Pick me up here around two o'clock. I should have something to go on by then." She shut the door, and wrapping her fur collar around her face against the wind, started across the street.

Two blocks from the Court House, I had to wait as a train rumbled through the middle of town, right across Main Street, dividing the town in two. My face was aching, so I let it slip back to my own button. I figured I was safe so long as I went quietly about my business and didn't attract any attention.

People gathered on the corner to either side of me waiting for the train to pass so they could cross the street. A few were well-dressed, but most were wearing last year's clothes, or maybe the year before. What got me, though, were their faces. Nobody was smiling. They all looked uniformly grim, like they should all be wearing black arm bands for a funeral. Maybe the "un" in Uniontown stood for "unhappy."

The caboose rumbled by, and Marge's confidence in my skills proved right. I spotted the Uniontown Public Library on the corner of Church Street and Beeson and found a parking space a street away. The Library was a smaller castle, complete with a turreted tower, built of the same blackened stone as the Court House. I was surprised that it wasn't an example of Carnegie's benevolence, but maybe his rivalry with Henry Clay Frick, J.V. Thompson, and the other Fayette County Coal Barons made him spend his money elsewhere.

I figured the library was apparently a church rectory at one time, based on the stained-glass windows and occasional alcove with a statue of one religious figure or another. The main room was lit with ceiling fixtures that told of better times and more generous donors. The reading chairs were worn, and empty. I guess the Uniontown Public Library had less tolerance for indigents than Squirrel Hill.

I stepped up to the desk, and a hefty woman gave me a stingy smile. "Can I help you?" I almost laughed out loud when I saw her. With her glasses down her nose and her dark hair wound in a bun so tight I figured it made her teeth hurt, she looked like the exaggerated version of a librarian you'd find in a comic strip with her finger to her lips shushing the Katzenjammer kids. The name plate on her desk identified her as Miss Martha Covington, emphasis on Miss.

"Do you have back issues of the local newspaper on file?"

"We have *The Morning Herald* for the past eight years upstairs in our archive. We also have the *Pittsburgh Post-Gazette* for the current six months. This week's newspapers are here in the reading room."

"Where do I find the archive, ma'am?"

"Miss." She pointed at her name plate. "Miss Covington."

"Okay, where do I find the archive, *Miss* Covington?"

"To your right on the second floor. You'll find Mister Davis there. He will help you." I thanked her and started to walk away, and she said, "By the way, there is no smoking allowed in the Library."

"Who said I smoked?"

"No one. But I can smell tobacco on your overcoat, and your fingers are stained with nicotine, if I'm not mistaken." She smiled smugly. "I read Agatha Christie, you see."

I nodded. "Yes, I see." I got away from her before she Agatha Christied my real identity.

Upstairs, I found a maze of shelves packed to the ceiling with books. At one end of the long room, a short man with a bald spot and a little pot belly sticking out of his suit jacket was unpacking one of a pile of boxes full of them.

"You Davis?"

He looked up from his work, blinking through thick lenses that magnified his watery blue eyes. "Yes. Can I help you?"

I don't know where "Can I help you?" got its start as the standard opening gambit for everyone from lingerie clerks to bureaucrats to second stringers everywhere, striking that delicate balance between authority and servitude. Miss Covington's version was at the far end of the authority scale. Davis's delivery was pure servitude, probably tongue lashed into him by the Dragon Lady downstairs. I almost wished he would have said, "Whattaya want, Mac?"

"I need to look through your newspaper files."

"Oh, certainly." He set down the book he was cataloguing. "It's very busy this week. J.J. Cunningham died a few months ago, and his family very generously donated his personal collection of books to the library."

"Well, if you'll just show me where the newspapers are, I'll get out of your way and let you get back to unpacking."

"This way." He led me to the far end of the room where a doorway opened into a smaller chamber whose shelves held big bound books. "Here is the newspaper collection. What year did you want to see?"

"1935 to start."

Davis hunched down and ran his finger along the spines of the books. "Here we are."

He pulled one of the monster volumes from the shelf and laid it on the table. "If you need another year, come and get me."

"I can just find it myself. No problem."

Davis frowned. "Oh, I can't let you do that." The absurdity of Davis not letting me do something was lost on him. "Miss Covington has strict rules about procedure. We have to remove and replace all of the files ourselves, or they may get mixed up, you see."

I reached in my pocket and peeled off a fiver. "I won't tell if you don't. Just between us guys, huh?" I slipped him the five, and he actually seemed to be thinking it over for a few seconds before he took it. He nodded and shuffled back to his boxes of books.

The newspaper volumes were less books than sheets of newsprint clamped into heavy cardboard binders. It was tedious work, scanning every page, but I fell into a rhythm of looking at headlines in descending order of type size from the biggest font to the smallest. I found six stories about moonshiners in 1935, and jotted down the names of the arrestees and the arrestors. Two of the later articles concerned trials, fines, and sentences. McNairy's name didn't show up in any of the crime stories, moonshine or otherwise. None of the other names rang a bell.

1934 was a little more fruitful. I found eleven articles about Revenuers and hillbillies, one set of stories three days in a row about a shootout near Kasparis in the Dunbar mountains that killed two locals and three Federals out of eight who raided a still out in the woods. Leafing from one page to another, I spotted a headline: Local Man to Race in Nazareth Speedway Classic. The article below it told of a local driver, twenty-year-old Donovan, "Rusty" Calhoun of Farmington. Calhoun grew up around the famous Uniontown Speedway in the twenties where his father Raymond Calhoun was a regular on the well-known track.

It all clicked; the driving skills, the moonshine mountain location, and especially the name. McNairy was keeping it Irish, maybe to show his Italian bosses that they didn't have a monopoly on big-ticket crime. A follow-up article reported Rusty Calhoun took third place at the track and brought home a five-hundred-dollar purse and a two-foot trophy. There was McNairy's wheel man, good enough to never get caught. I cracked 1933 to see if there was a mention of Calhoun, and was halfway through the papers when I heard footsteps on the stairs: one pair.

I heard whispering from the next room and it set off alarm bells. I gathered my notes and slipped them into my pocket. Lucky for me I thought to look out the window. A cop car pulled up to the curb and four uniforms jumped out. All of them drew their guns. I opened the window and chanced sticking my head out. I saw all four run up the steps to the entrance. No one waited on the sidewalk. I guess everybody wanted to be in on the big pinch; just plain stupid. I quietly shut the door to the archive room—I was lucky it swung inward—and grabbed one of the tall, heavy racks. It took some muscle, but I was able to tip it forward so that it jammed the door.

The Library building was cut stone, and the striking was wide enough for my fingers. I hadn't climbed up or down the side of a building in years, but I managed with a few broken nails and no broken bones. I dropped to the sidewalk to the stares of a couple of pedestrians, and I intentionally ran away from the street where I'd parked the Packard. I figured the gawkers would tell the flatfeet, "He went that-away," so I ran a block and doubled back through an alley. I got in the car and switched my face.

Just for laughs, I drove past the Library in time to see the befuddled coppers come rushing out the door, heads swiveling. One of them noticed me, stared for a second, didn't see Ike Mars, and then went back to swiveling. Oh, that Miss Covington; Agatha Christie would be proud. So would Mack Sennett.

I had another hour before I picked up Marge, so I parked the Packard a street over from Main and went into the Titlow Hotel. The Titlow was old school, lots of oak in the woodwork and wainscoting, and high stamped tin ceilings. A bar and a dining room ran parallel from the Main Street entrance halfway to the back of the building. I opted for the bar.

"Bourbon and draft."

The bartender drew my beer and poured the shot. I dropped the shot glass into the foamy mug, and he laughed. "From Pittsburgh, huh?"

"No, actually, Toledo."

He grunted and moved down the bar to refill somebody else's drink. Habits. They give a guy away just as sure as his birthmarks, scars, or dimples. And that ain't all. Once, when I was undercover wearing somebody else's face, I stopped at Blind Eddie's news stand on Forbes for a paper. I made my voice hoarse, and asked for the *Press*. Eddie took my nickel and said.

"Can't fool me, Mister Mars. You're wearing those squeaky shoes of yours."

I drank my beer and watched out the big front window as cop cars ran up and down Main Street, spinners flashing. Sometimes the best way to outrun the Law is to just sit still.

Behind the bar I saw framed photos of race cars on an oval track and drivers posing in or behind cars with numbers on the hoods and sides. One of the photos had a sign in the background that said Uniontown Speedway. I called the bartender over. "Were those photos taken around here?"

"Yes, sir. Mister Titlow, the owner of this hotel was one of the men who invested in building the track, and people came from all over the country to race and to watch. As many as fifty thousand would come. They built the Speedway after the Highway Department outlawed the hill climb races up Summit Mountain."

"I recognize Barney Oldfield from news photos, but I don't know the others. Any of them local?"

He pointed to a picture of a driver in leather helmet and goggles holding a trophy. "That guy, Ray Calhoun. He was a good driver, and he might have gone on to be national champion, but he got killed near the end of the War."

"Is that his kid?" I pointed to a young boy standing beside the car with a grin as wide as his father's.

"Yeah, that's Rusty. He was as good as his old man or better. The Speedway closed in '22, but he went on the national circuit for a while, then he just dropped out of sight. Haven't heard anything about him in a couple of years."

"Thanks for the info." I put two bucks on the bar and headed for the street. I pulled up to the Court House as the clock in the tower chimed two. Marge came out and crossed the street in the blustery wind, holding her hat down with one hand, and holding her skirt down with the other.

She climbed into the car and shut the door. "Got some names for you."

"One of them Calhoun?"

"You've been busy too."

I pulled away from the curb and drove around the block two times while I filled her in on the day's adventures. Then it was her turn.

"I found court records for Duncan Calhoun and his son Raymond when they were prosecuted for moonshining ten years back. The old man ran the still and the son drove the tanker. Duncan was born in—can you guess— County Cork, Ireland, just like Liam McNairy, but Raymond was home grown. I located birth records for him and a more recent branch of the family tree, Donovan."

"Rusty."

She nodded. "Apparently. Now that we agree on the name, I can try the Assessor's office, check the tax rolls, then try the Recorder of Deeds. If I'm lucky, I can find out where the Calhoun family plants their corn."

"They just let you paw through the records?"

"It's public information. I get the impression that the Calhouns aren't connected, so nobody gives a damn if somebody snoops. And beside my press card from the newspaper, I have credentials that are Presidential."

"George Washington strikes again."

"More like Hamilton and Jackson."

"What corruption. I'm shocked."

"Don't be. It's a way of life around here."

I pulled up in front of the Court House and she went back inside. The lead seemed slim, but it was more than I had when I woke up. If Rusty Calhoun was Irish Frank's getaway driver, the Calhoun family farm might just be the hiding place where Frank stashed the mysterious Hudson.

While Marge was working her magic with the public records, I got the car gassed up and drove around looking for a clothing store. On Morgantown Street, I found a dress shop with the name Axelrod's over the door in fancy script. The dress on the mannequin in the window would look great on Marge—okay, if it came in her size, but give me some room for imagination. At three o'clock, I picked her up in front of the Court House.

"Okay, head for Route 40 East. According to the County tax rolls, Calhoun's place is up in the mountains, eighteen acres off Flat Rock Road in Markleysburg."

"Know how to get there?"

"Buy a map."

"While I do that, I have another job for you." I stopped the Packard in front of Axelrod's. I peeled a wad of cash off my roll and didn't bother to count it. I pushed it into her hand. " We might be done tomorrow, or we might be sawing on this log for another week. Go in there and buy whatever you need."

She didn't even blink. She stuffed the bills in her purse and opened the door. "Half an hour."

That's my Marge.

It took me longer to find a map and get two conflicting sets of directions from two different pump jockeys than it did for her to shop for clothes. She was watching out the store window when I pulled up. Marge came out of Axelrod's with her arms full of bundles and a hatbox dangling by a ribbon from her index finger.

"You made a real haul, didn't you?" I laughed as she tossed the packages in the back seat.

She said, "Hold out your hand." I did, and she dropped two dimes, a nickel, and three pennies in it. "There's your change."

Like I said, that's my Marge.

Markleysburg was about fifteen miles east of Uniontown, over the Summit, the highest peak in the chunk of the Alleghenies that cut across the corner of Fayette County. Looking at the map, I could see why it was a good location for moonshining. The little town, which was not much more than a combination post office, gas station, and grocery store surrounded by a handful of houses, lay in a nook in the mountains that was five miles from the West Virginia border and ten from Maryland. The hills were crisscrossed with dirt roads on nobody's map that would allow moonshiners easy access to interstate commerce. The land surrounding Markleysburg was largely second-growth forest and hardscrabble farms wrestled out of the rocky soil.

"So, what do we do, Mars? Knock on the door and tell Duncan Calhoun we're looking for a missing getaway car full of diamonds and does he have one in his barn?"

"I'd guess we have to play it cagey. These mountain guys all keep a shotgun behind the door. Maybe you could be a damsel in distress with a broken-down car and use his phone while I take a look in the corn crib."

"What if he likes my looks and wants me to stay for dinner and drinks?"

"That's why you have a gun in your purse. We don't know if he's alone out there. You didn't find any info about a wife did you?"

"Nope. There are limits to everything, including information."

We drove up the Summit, and the Packard handled the steep grade pretty well. The big V-8 kept us rolling at a steady thirty-five in second gear. This was the site for the hill climb races the bartender at the Titlow was talking about. In the other direction, cars crept down the grade, to prevent burning up their brakes and freewheeling into Hopwood at the bottom.

The mountain was snow covered, but the road was still clear for the most part. Near the peak the road took a broad curve and gave us a view of the valley below. Dark clouds stretched from one end of the sky to the other. It would snow soon, and it would snow big.

At the crest, a hotel that looked like an oversized mansion snuggled into the hillside as if it had been dropped from the sky. The sign said "Mount Summit Inn." It also said "closed for the season."

"That's too bad," I said. "That would be conveniently close."

"Maybe we'll find something else along the way."

The road was a giant roller coaster of steep hills and deep valleys lined with a dense growth of trees and brush, white with snow. I decided that we'd better reconnoiter and get off the mountain as quick as we could, before we got snowed in for the winter.

We passed Flat Rock Road once and had to turn around. The sign was almost invisible behind an untrimmed stand of pines. Flat rock road was level, running the top of a ridge, but as curvy as a rattlesnake, and edged with ditches that could swallow a bus. I drove slowly, and Marge and I watched the mailboxes. The snow had started falling in thick fat gobs, and the wipers had to struggle to keep up.

"We must be in West Virginia by now," Marge said.

"Seems more like Minnesota."

"Hey! There it is." Marge pointed to a mailbox at the mouth of a lane. The snow covered half of the name Calhoun, and in another five minutes, would have obscured it completely.

"Okay, now we know. We'd better get this heap turned around and get back to 40. I don't want to drive off the road in the dark in this snow . I found a wide spot in the road a half mile farther and did a street turn. By the time we got back to the highway, the shadows in the trees looked like they were brushed in with India Ink.

The Packard fishtailed when we pulled onto 40, and I could see it was going to be a long, slow ride. I was glad I filled the tank in Uniontown. Driving the mountain road was tricky. If I lost traction going up one of those steep hills and slid back down into the trough, I'd be stuck. I had to go faster than I really wanted to down one hill to have the momentum to carry the heavy car over the next one. It didn't help that I could see only about twenty feet in front of me. I hadn't seen lights from another car in either direction for miles.

"Mars, look out." I saw them the same instant Marge did, a half dozen tawny shapes darted across the headlights, a herd of white- tailed deer. If I hit the brake, I'd lose my push and maybe go into a skid that would take me off the road into the trees. I just kept rolling.

Five of the deer cleared the front of the Packard. The last one wasn't so lucky. The car hit it with a solid thump, and it rolled over the left front fender and back onto the road. Through the side window, I saw it get up and run off to join its buddies. The left headlight winked out. Great, now I was driving half blind on top of everything else.

"This is getting better by the minute," Marge said. She lit a cigarette for herself and one for me.

We cleared another ridge and I saw the big yellow sign: Dangerous grade—descend in lowest gear. I hit the brakes and the car slewed sideways to a stop.

"What are you doing?"

"There's no way we'll make it down the mountain tonight. I pointed through the windshield at the shadowy bulk of the Mount Summit Inn. "No Room Service, babe, but I'm sure we can scare up enough blankets to keep us from freezing 'til sunup."

I pulled the car into the hotel driveway and under the portico. A broad set of steps led to a veranda that spanned the front of the dark building. We got out of the car, and stood for minute, listening. A blanket of heavy snow has a muffling effect that soaks up sound like a blotter soaks up ink. All we could hear was the quiet hiss of the falling blizzard.

As we climbed the steps, I saw a sign that read, "Porch accommodations, breakfast included, two dollars. Sleeping bags available." The Depression wasn't quite over yet. The double doors that led to the lobby were locked, of course, but that never slowed me down too much. I picked the lock, and in a minute we were inside the darkened hotel.

I flicked my cigarette lighter and took a quick look around. The lobby was as big as a church, two stories tall. Directly across from the entrance, a grand staircase led to a balcony and the second floor. To the left of the stairs, I saw the reception desk and the bell captain's station. I blew out a breath and saw it in the chilly air. After the warmth of the car, the lobby was downright cold.

Sofas and chairs were covered in white dust drapes and gave the interior the same look as the snow covered bushes out front. A rough stone fireplace took up a big part of the wall to the right. There was kindling and some firewood in a wrought iron cradle on the flagstone hearth. At least I wouldn't have to break up the furniture for fuel.

Brass candlesticks stood at either end of the mantel. I lit the candles and they threw a soft glow over the place. Marge hugged herself. "For God's sake, get a fire going, Mars, before I turn into an ice cube."

I splintered a piece of the kindling in the grate, tee-peed some more around it then built a pyramid of firewood around the center. Just like I did in the Boy Scouts. A flick of the lighter, the kindling caught, and the fire was on its way.

We pulled a settee in front of the hearth and sat down without bothering to take off the dust cover. "Oh, hell."

Smoke was curling from the fireplace into the room. I'd forgotten to open the damper. I was kneeling on the hearth looking for the lever when a voice behind me said, "Flue lever's on the left end."

I jumped up and my hand instinctively went for my gun. I heard a pair of hammers cock and recognized the sound of a Remington .12 gauge.

"Easy," the voice said. "Put your hands down, friend. Nobody's mad at anybody. You just surprised me, is all."

A man stepped from the shadows. He was short, about five foot two and wiry. His face looked unfinished, features indistinct, like a rubber stamp on the third try without inking up. His eyes were little dark beads peeking through squinty eyelids. I guessed his mother was on the bottle nine months before he was. He was wearing a fur hat with ear flaps and one of those red and black checked wool coats that hunters seem to favor. He could have been thirty, forty, or fifty. It was hard to tell.

I was right about the Remington. He held it loosely, finger on the triggers, right hand under the twin barrels and the stock tucked in his armpit. He was a lefty.

"I know why you folks are here. Question is, who are you?"

"Just a couple of travelers stranded by the snow. I'm Ike Williams, and this is my wife Marge."

He nodded. "How'd you get in?"

"The door was open."

"No, it wasn't."

I turned my palms up in a "you got me" gesture. "It was, after I picked the lock."

He laughed and let down the shotgun. I noticed He didn't let down the hammers. "Yeah, I figured. My name's Henry Stutz. I'm the caretaker."

"Well, Henry, now that we're here, can we stay?"

"Wouldn't be very Christian of me to turn you out on a night like this. I suppose you could."

"'Could' isn't 'can'. How about five bucks?"

"Oh, hell, Ike, give him ten," Marge said.

"Like the lady said, and for that, I'll throw in supper. I got plenty on the stove."

I learned a long time ago to never carry all my cash in one pocket. I pulled a small sheaf of bills from my raincoat and thumbed through it 'til I found a ten. I'd have to know Henry a whole lot better before I let him see my main roll.

Henry leaned into the fireplace, and I heard the clank of a heavy steel damper. He took the ten from me and smiled. His teeth, such as they were, were the shade of brown a lifetime of chewing tobacco gives you. He twitched his head to the side. "Come on. My place is in the back."

He led us through a hallway and threw a wall switch. We were in the hotel kitchen. The place was immaculate. Every surface gleamed and not one item lay out of place on any of the counters or in the sink.

We crossed the kitchen and went through a doorway to another corridor. At its end a door stood ajar. Henry pushed the door inward and we followed him inside. He switched on the light, and we found ourselves in a small two-room apartment. A table and two chairs sat to one side, a sink and small gas stove to the other. I couldn't see what was in the pot on the stove, but it smelled pretty good. So did the coffee. A small radio on the counter was playing some cowboy tune about riding the prairie.

"Made stew tonight. I'll get you a couple plates." He turned a dial on the stove, and a halo of blue flame sprang up under the pot. "Be back in a minute." He disappeared into the hallway.

I looked around the room. It was as clean as the kitchen. Through the open door, I could see a neatly made bed in the next room. Whatever else may be wrong with Henry Stutz, he was a good housekeeper. He came back from the hotel kitchen with plates and cups. All were emblazoned in red with an Old English S, the crest of the Summit Inn.

"Hope you like rabbit." He set the plates on the stove and spooned out a generous serving for each of us then carried the plates to the table.

Neither of us had ever eaten rabbit stew before, but we agreed it was delicious.

"In the really cold weather, I'll make a big batch, eat what I want for supper, then put the lid on the pot and set it out in the sun room where it's as cold as the outside. The food freezes, and when I'm ready to eat again, I just put it on the stove and thaw it out."

Marge and I looked at each other. "Don't worry, folks. I just made that batch today."

"Come on. My place is in the back."

"You shot the rabbits?"

"Right out the back door. They run all over the place when it's not busy.

"I can think of a few deer you might want to cook, one in particular."

"Yeah, there's a bunch of them too. 'Hoofed rats' my daddy used to call them when they'd eat all the greens out of his garden. They're pretty good eating too. I like venison."

He poured coffee for us. "Sorry I don't have cream, but I do have sugar if you want it."

We both shook our heads. I'm a firm believer that coffee should be strong and taste like coffee, not some ice cream parlor treat. Marge agreed with me. He poured three cups and waited until Marge and I took ours before he took one for himself. Call me overly cautious, but it reassured me that he wasn't slipping us a Mickey.

"When did the hotel close for the year?"

"End of October. Of course, business slows down then, and we started closing floors a couple of weeks ago. Strip the beds, roll up the mattresses, and shut off the water so the pipes don't freeze. But there's still heat on the first floor. I can fix you up a room so you don't have to sleep on the rug in the lobby."

He brought another chair from the bedroom and joined us at the table. The stew was delicious, and the coffee was strong, just what Marge and I both needed. When we were done, Henry took the dishes to the kitchen. He was gone for a few minutes, and when he came back, he had sheets and blankets over his arm. "If you want, you can come with me and I'll make up your bed."

We followed him through the eerie silence of the hotel around the corner from the registration desk. Henry switched on lights as we went. The walls were hung with paintings, real ones, not lithographs and antique furniture that was probably worth more than I'd earn in a lifetime. I understood why Henry lived on the site and why he carried a shotgun.

He opened a door and flicked the light switch. I was surprised, Feature for feature, the room was every bit as elegant as our suites in the William Penn. The big difference was the double bed, a four-poster with its blue striped mattress rolled at the foot on top of a set of coiled springs. Henry turned the valve on the radiator and I heard steam hissing. He unrolled the mattress and set the bedding on it then he stepped into the bathroom. I heard water running in the bathtub.

"The water heater's on year 'round, but you'll have to let the tap run a while 'til the hot water gets here." He started to make the bed, and Marge stopped him.

"I'll do that. Maybe you two could get our things from the car."

I followed Henry outside. The snow was still falling and looked to be about ten inches deep on the driveway. Henry pointed a torch at the broken headlight. "I see what you meant about the deer."

"Yeah, well the car got hurt worse than he did." I looked at the sky. "How long do you think it'll snow?"

"Hard to tell this time of year."

"Will the highway be clear tomorrow?"

"Likely so. Some people chipped in some time back to buy the Township a plow truck, a big old Oshkosh four-wheel-drive, and they usually tackle the Summit first."

"Times like these, who had the cash for something like that?" I said, although I thought I already knew the answer.

"I'm not one to tell tales, Mister Williams, but that happened during Prohibition. I heard it was bootleggers wanted to make sure the roads were clear when they had a delivery."

It made sense. Canadian whiskey floated across Lake Erie and from there, it was trucked south as far as Maryland and Virginia. I knew a grand gesture like that couldn't have sprung strictly from a sense of civic duty.

"If you have chains, I can help you put them on."

"I'll have to look in the trunk. This is my brother's car."

"I hope he ain't too mad having to repaint it again."

I blinked. "Huh?"

"Where the deer hit, I can see a different color under the maroon."

The guy looked like a dimwit, but he didn't miss much. "I'll have to ask him. They have deer in Center County too."

I opened the trunk, something I hadn't done before. If Art McCurdy opened it, he never said so, but if he did and he saw what was inside, he figured it was best left unmentioned. When Henry shined his light into it, we saw a pair of riot guns, two bullet-proof vests and a Thompson submachine gun.

"I guess you don't have any chains, huh?"

I had to think fast. I shook my head. "Here's the score, Henry." I reached into my pocket and pulled out one of the badges. The brass glowed in the beam of his torch. "The lady and I are undercover cops. Some members of John Dillinger's old gang pulled a bank heist in Pittsburgh. The word is they're holed up someplace around here, and we're trying to find them before they pull another job or get away clean."

He looked down at his feet for a minute like he was thinking it over and maybe wishing he didn't leave his shotgun back in his room.

"This weather's put us in a real bind, Henry. The question is, can we count on you to help us?"

He raised his head for a three count while he looked me in the eye then gave a single sharp nod of determination. "You bet, Mister Williams."

"That's Lieutenant Williams, and Sergeant Smith, just so you'll know."

He chuckled. "I figured you two weren't man and wife when I saw you weren't wearing rings. When I saw the guns, I thought you were crooks, you know, like Bonnie and Clyde. Then you showed me the badges, and I thought, hell, these people are Revenuers and you were after my cousins."

"No, we're not here for your cousins, Henry, and I didn't ask." I shut the trunk. "We'll wait to see what the weather's like tomorrow. Maybe I won't need chains."

We took the suitcases and the bags from Axelrod's to the room. Marge had made the bed and was warming her hands over the clanking radiator. "Thanks for your help, Henry. Sergeant Smith and I can take it from here." Marge blinked but knew better than to say anything. "You take the bed, Sarge. I'll take the chair." She nodded.

"One last thing, Henry; I have to check in with my superiors. Is the phone working?"

"Yep, if the lines haven't come down in this snow. Come on, Lieutenant. I'll open up the office for you."

Henry stepped out into the hall and Marge made a face. She mouthed the word "Sergeant?" and rolled her eyes. I shrugged. "I'll call the office and I'll be right back."

The hotel office was around the corner from the lobby behind an imposing oak door. Henry took a big ring of keys from his coat pocket and thumbed through them. To me, they all looked alike, but there was a lock in the place for every one of them. He found the key that he wanted and opened the door.

Henry stepped in and stood for a minute, almost reverent, as if he had stepped into a cathedral. By his attitude, I half expected him to take off his hat.

"Is this the manager's office? Pretty nice."

"No," Henry almost whispered, "It's the Mister's office." He said it with the same deference as Irish families often refer to their patriarch as "Himself."

The windowless walls were paneled in the same dark oak as the door, and covered with photos of a tall, lean man in golf clothes swinging a driver. No pictures of wife or kids. A display frame showed off a fancy putter. The room was dominated by a desk the size of Montana with nothing on it but a telephone and a brass name plate that read, "Donald V. Hannabeck, Owner. Behind the desk was a high-backed leather chair that looked more like a throne, dwarfing the two visitor chairs that seemed to cower on the other side. One more little kingdom.

"There's the phone."

I started around the desk, and Henry put up a hand to stop me. "Uh, Lieutenant, the Mister doesn't like anybody else to sit in his chair."

"No problem; I'll stand." I picked up the handset and was about to dial the number when I noticed Henry was still waiting in the doorway. He was probably watching to make sure I didn't breathe on anything, or disturb the nap of the carpet.

I called Mason's apartment. It was unlikely he'd be in the office that late. The phone rang and rang. I was about to give up when he finally answered.

"Yeah."

"Captain Cutter, this is Lieutenant Williams."

Mason laughed so loud that I practically shoved the phone into my ear so that Henry wouldn't hear it. "I'm calling from the Mount Summit Inn in Farmington. Sergeant Smith and I have a line on the suspects, but the snow is causing us problems."

"I'll bet." He chuckled at the other end. "Marge the Sarge, huh? Bet she loves that moniker. Here's a news flash for you. I was at the County Jail today delivering a bail skip, when who strolls in wearing manacles between two harness bulls but Irish Frank McNairy. He's holed up in the executive suite in the jail under guard. The bookies are running odds on how long he stays alive."

"And Jeffers?"

"He was on hand to greet the visiting dignitary. And guess who showed up on either elbow: LaSorda and Vanner. People in this town are either stupid, blind, or so used to crooked it looks like plumb."

"That turns the heat up a notch, doesn't it?"

Mason grunted. "You need help up there?"

"Sure, but you know how surveillance works. Hard to shake a tail."

"Right. Czap still has eyes on me, but I'll see what I can manage."

I hung up and I swear Henry breathed a sigh of relief when I left "the Mister's" den. We all have to answer to somebody, I guess, but I was glad

I didn't have Donald V. Hannabeck for a boss. Two weeks in, and I'd probably go to the chair for beating him to death with his five iron.

"Well, thanks for everything, Henry. Your cooperation is greatly appreciated by the Department." I laid it on thick.

"Glad to help, Lieutenant." He seemed to revere the title; not quite "the Mister," but a rung or two up the ladder.

"I can find my way back. See you in the morning."

"I think I'll go sit in the lobby 'til the fire goes out and I can close the damper." He handed me the room key and walked away. Halfway down the hall, he was whistling what I made out to be "Streets of Laredo."

Back in the room, Marge was sitting on the bed, her pistol beside her on the blanket. "Sergeant? I couldn't be a lieutenant like you?"

"Marge the Sarge," I said, stealing a line from Mason. "It seemed to fit."

She threw a pillow at me. "You jerk."

I spread my hands in apology. "I had to tell Henry something to get him on board after he looked in the trunk." I filled her in on the whole story, but I kept my voice down in case Henry was out in the hall with his ear to the door.

When I finished, Marge said, "So what do you think McNairy's hearing means?"

"I don't know. He and Jeffers may be at odds, or they might be on the same team by now. Hard to tell. But if they're going to work together, we'd better hustle to find the Hudson before McNairy leads Jeffers to it."

"Yeah? Well if we're going to sleep here tonight, you'd better lock the door. "

"A lot of good that'll do. Stutz has a key to every room in the hotel."

"Then put the chain on the door and shove that dresser in front of it. I don't want that weirdo to cut our throats in our sleep so we end up in his stewpot."

Marge and I slept in our clothes with the light on and our guns handy. The room was warm enough for me, but not for her, so I let her double the blankets over her and pulled my raincoat up to my chin. I didn't bother looking outside. Either it was still snowing or it wasn't, and knowing would just make me think about tomorrow and keep me awake.

XXII

When I woke up, it was just getting light outside. I parted the curtains to see a pale pink dawn in the works. Another four or five inches had fallen overnight; more snow later maybe, but not at the moment. Our room was on the ground level, and when I looked down, I saw footprints in the snow leading up to the window, milling around a little, then back around the building. Nothing to see here, I thought, but I was still glad we pulled down the shade.

I tried to get out of bed gently, but the creaking springs woke up Sleeping Beauty. "Good Lord, Mars, what time is it?"

I looked at my watch. "Six thirty. Sleep enough?"

"I never sleep enough," Marge said through a yawn. " She got out of bed, went into the bathroom, and closed the door behind her. "See you in a half hour."

I went out and strolled down the hall in search of Henry and coffee. I knocked and heard the radio through the door. The nasal voice of some Bible thumping preacher reminded me that it was Sunday.

Henry opened the door dressed in the same clothes he had on the night before. So was I, but his were probably the same clothes he'd had on for the last month. The smell of coffee was enough to set aside any further criticism.

"Come on in. Pull up a chair."

He poured coffee for us. "Sergeant Smith coming too?"

"Not just yet."

I picked up the cup, warming my hands around it.

"Want a nip to go with it?" He didn't wait for an answer, but instead, got up from his chair and took a Mason jar from the overhead cabinet. "Since you ain't a Revenuer, I guess it's okay to trot out the old Mountain Dew. He unscrewed the lid and poured a healthy dollop into his cup. He looked at me and raised his eyebrows. I nodded and he poured as much in mine.

He took a gulp of his spiked coffee, and I took a sip of mine. If Henry's mother drank this stuff while he was in the womb, it went a long way to explain his looks.

"That always gets me rolling on a cold winter day," he cackled.

"Did it snow much more last night?"

"Maybe another inch. I was asleep before it quit, but when I looked out, it wasn't much deeper than before. The plow's been down the mountain already, so it'll be back up this way before too long."

"You said something about having chains."

"Yep, have some in the tool shed. I can help you put 'em on."

"Go ahead and drink your coffee. There's no big rush. If I'm going to do that, I'd better change my clothes." I took the hillbilly coffee with me back to the room. I knocked and announced myself before I turned the key so Marge wouldn't shoot me through the door. I pushed the door inward, and it snapped to a stop at the end of the security chain.

"Keep your pants on."

"Actually, I was thinking of taking them off and putting on another pair." The door slammed in my face, I heard the snick of the chain, and then it opened to reveal Marge in a green pullover sweater and pleated khaki slacks *a la* Marlene Deitrich.

"I decided if we were going traipsing off into the woods, I'd better wear something other than a cocktail dress. Axelrod's was very accommodating."

"Good thinking."

I opened my suitcase and pulled out my slacks and shirt. I should have told the William Penn no starch. When I put my clothes on, they felt like cardboard. I strapped on my rig and checked my revolver. Still full up, which made sense since I hadn't fired it for a couple of days.

When I came back to Henry's room, he was still at the table drinking what looked like another full cup of coffee. The bottle was still sitting on the table, so I figured this cup was just as potent as the last.

"I was thinking," he said. Lord, I thought, what could he be thinking about? "Where is it you have to go?"

I thought about telling him or not, and since he knew the area and the roads, not to mention the people, telling him won the argument. "Flat Rock Road."

"That probably ain't been plowed yet." He cocked his head and looked at me sidewise. "I can give you chains, but you might do better with Mabel."

"Mabel?"

"She's my truck."

Henry took me outside to a row of garage bays and opened the first pair of doors. "Here's Mabel," he said proudly.

Mabel was a 1918 International farm truck with a dump bed. The truck was an odd shade of greenish blue with black running boards and fenders in the front and open wheels in the back. The cab was squared off like an old Model T Ford , and the front sported sealed beam headlights flanking a flat radiator with a winged cap topped by a temperature gauge. Mabel gleamed in the early morning light; Henry tended his truck with the same meticulous care he did the hotel kitchen and his apartment.

"She rides high, and I've never gotten stuck, no matter how deep the snow."

I weighed our options. The tires on the Packard were no match for the deep chevron mud treads on the truck. Unlike the low-slung car, the truck had good clearance. Its running boards were a good foot off the ground, and the frame had little or nothing to drag on the deepest drifts.

"I guess Mabel's our best bet. Anything I need to know about the gears?"

Henry's affable grin snapped off his face, replaced with a look bordering on indignation. "Oh, no, Lieutenant. You can't drive Mabel. Nobody drives Mabel but me." His tone probably would have been the same if I said I wanted to make love to his wife, if he ever had one. "I'll take you wherever you have to go."

Marge and I had to get to Calhoun's farm, and we had to get away again. I didn't like the idea of involving a civilian, but I couldn't trust the Packard or my winter driving skills to pull it off. "I understand. Okay, Henry, I guess I'll have to deputize you, then. Raise your right hand."

Henry's eyes shone with excitement. "Gee, just like *Gangbusters* on the radio."

As I swore Henry in with a bogus made up oath, I thought about the irony of having another country boy as my wheel man to go after Irish Frank and his.

I collected Marge, and we decided to leave our bags in the room. If we got away with this operation, they'd still be there when we came back. If we didn't, it wouldn't matter much. Marge saw the truck, and instead of her usual wisecracking, she said, "She's a beauty. Perfect." Henry beamed.

He cranked the motor by hand, and Mabel chugged into life. By the time we set out, the plow truck hadn't made its way back up the Summit, but the sun was up, and the sky was an almost cloudless blue. The snow was at least a foot deep in the road, maybe more, and as wary as I was of Henry's involvement, I was glad he was driving.

The truck had a lot more traction than the Packard, and Henry didn't have to roller-coaster the hills and valleys. He kept a steady twenty miles per hour, and the truck's tires didn't slip once. Henry kept a running commentary, some fact or gossip about every farm we passed and where every snowed-in lane led.

We turned onto Flat Rock Road and found unbroken snow. "Nobody's been in or out of here today," Henry said, around his wad of tobacco. "You didn't tell me exactly how far we were going."

"About two miles down the road," Marge told him. "The Calhoun farm."

Henry nodded. "I know where it is. Old man Calhoun's a mean one. He's an old moonshiner hates Revenuers and shoots at trespassers; won't let anybody hunt on his land." He grinned, "But I know a way to sneak in, shoot a few squirrels, and get back out again without getting caught."

"He doesn't hear your gun?" I said.

"Nope, he's almost stone deaf."

"Anybody else live with him?"

"No, his Missus died a few years back, and now he's by himself."

"Maybe, if our tip is right, he's not alone now."

Mabel clawed her way through the heavy snow at a steady pace for a few more minutes until we reached the mailbox at the end of the lane. "There she is. What do I do?"

"You said you had a way of getting on and off the property without being seen. Maybe you could show me the way, and then Sergeant Smith can walk in by the lane. He's not likely to shoot at a woman."

"You hope," she snorted.

"She'll tell him her car's stuck and keep him occupied while I look around."

"But what'll I do?" Henry said.

"You'll stay near the mailbox and keep Mabel running so we can make a fast getaway if we run into trouble. If the Dillinger gang is holed up at the farm, we can't take them on by ourselves. We'll need reinforcements."

"Yes, sir, Lieutenant, I'll do what you say."

Henry drove the truck to a spot a half mile up the road. "That break in the trees is the head of a path that winds through the woods for a ways and comes out behind Calhoun's place. You oughta be able to get there without him spotting you." I climbed out of the truck and took one of the riot guns from behind the seat. "I wish you could take the other one with you," I told Marge."

"Where would I hide it?" She gave me a worried frown and said, "Be careful, Ike."

"You too, Marge."

I stood a while at the head of the trail, watching Mabel chug away through the snow. I gritted my teeth and started plodding through the white stuff. There were plenty of oaks and elms, bare limbed in the winter, but there were as many pines, giving me some cover. The snow started falling again, and that was a good thing; it would cover my tracks a little bit and maybe Calhoun wouldn't know that I'd been there. My feet were freezing; wingtips weren't snow shoes.

Just as Henry said, in about twenty minutes, I topped a rise, and smelled wood smoke first, then I found myself looking at a cluster of buildings, all grey unpainted wood nestled in a bowl-shaped valley. I counted six altogether, including the outhouse; a barn, a corn crib, a one-story house that looked to be little more than a cabin with smoke wiping from chimney, and two good-sized sheds. If I was lucky, McNairy's Hudson was in one of them.

I saw Marge coming down the lane from the other direction, floundering in the snow, and I hated myself for involving her, but at this point, knowing all that she knew, her life was on the line as much as mine was, and we had to pull together to get through this alive.

I circled behind the house and started for the barn. It was a big one, lots of room to hide a car. I rolled the door open a foot or so and slipped inside. I found cows in stalls, a loft full of hay, and no Hudson. I kicked away the straw on the floor and saw the boards were pegged planks, none of them loose to lead to some underground hideaway.

The first equipment shed had a tractor, a disc harrow and a rack of tools, scythes, rakes, hoes and such on one wall. In one corner under a tarp, I found a fifty-gallon tank and coils of copper tubing; moonshine still materials, but they were covered in dust and cobwebs, unused in years.

The second shed was a makeshift garage with a red Plymouth coupe parked over a grease pit. The car had the number twenty-three stenciled in white on the doors, along with the name Rusty Calhoun in fancy script. A workbench on the side was stocked with hand tools. I was right. Here was where Rusty worked on his cars. The Plymouth and the tools were as dusty as the unused still.

I was coming out of the shed when I saw Marge headed in my direction. Behind her was a tall man in a canvas hunting coat and a leather ball cap. He had rimless glasses hooked on his big ears, a three-day growth of grizzled whiskers on his cheeks, green rubber boots on his feet, and a bolt-action rifle aimed at Marge's head.

"Set down that scattergun and come out real slow if you don't this gal to get hurt." His voice was loud, as they often are with people hard of hearing. "Ain't telling you twice."

I threw the riot gun out the door, and it disappeared into a gun-shaped hole in the snow. I raised my hands and held them palms forward to show they were empty. My mind raced. Who could I turn into that would hold off the old man?

I concentrated hard on the photo I saw over the bar in the Titlow, Rusty Calhoun as a kid. I could feel my face trying to move, but it was like trying to lift five hundred pounds off the floor. Pain shot from my jaw to my scalp. My face wouldn't change. Maybe it was the cold, or maybe I just wore out the forty-three muscles in my face twisting and molding them into shapes that didn't belong there so many times in so few days. The why didn't matter; I was up the creek and my paddle was floating away.

"I'm sorry, Ike." Marge said. "Snuffy Smith here's smarter than he looks, or just more suspicious."

"Think I'm a fool?" He snorted. "Donnie Boy called me on the telephone, said he'd be coming and to watch out for strangers." He jerked his head at Marge." Send a woman in to keep me busy while you sneak around and find my still."

Calhoun's train of thought was easily derailed. If he had a still, it was out in the woods some place; either that or the old man was just living in the past. I played the first card that came to mind. "We aren't Revenuers, Mister Calhoun. Donnie Boy sent us to check on the car."

"If Donnie Boy sent you, where is he?" I noticed that he didn't say, "What car?"

"He's hiding out 'til it's safe. He just wants us to make sure the car's okay."

Calhoun's eyes seemed to glaze over. "He's a good grandson, my Donnie Boy—sends me money every month so's I don't have to make moon no more to feed myself." It made sense. McNairy couldn't chance law enforcement turning the farm inside out looking for a still and maybe finding the Hudson. And if it wasn't really Rusty on the phone, the old hillbilly was so hard of hearing he wouldn't have known the difference.

Calhoun suddenly snapped back into focus. "No more chit-chat. You two head for the house. I'm right behind you." Up close, I could see the merry-go-rounds spinning in the old man's eyeballs. I decided to cooperate for the moment and wait for a chance to get that rifle away from him.

Marge and I plodded down the hill toward the house. I took a chance that Calhoun couldn't hear me if I whispered. "Maybe if you stumble in the snow and fall down out of the line of fire, I can get to my .38 and shoot him before—" We both heard the sound at the same time, a mix of rumbling exhaust and the whine of spinning tires. A big, dark sedan was fighting its way down the lane.

"No more chit-chat. You two head for the house. I'm right behind you."

Calhoun marched us down the hill to the house and held us at gunpoint as the car, a green Pontiac, finally got as far as it could and bogged down a hundred feet away. The doors opened, and I wasn't surprised to see District Attorney Ambrose Jeffers along with Irish Frank McNairy, Vanner, and LaSorda. "Hail, hail, the gang's all here," Marge quipped under her breath.

They were all dressed in suits and topcoats. Nobody brought galoshes, so they had a tough time getting up the hill. Vanner fell on his ass once, and I would have laughed if I didn't have a thirty-ought-six pointed at my head.

Irish Frank looked none the worse for wear despite three years in the joint. I figured Jeffers saw to it that he got royal treatment and made sure Frank didn't get shanked in the yard by one of his fellow inmates before he could lead Jeffers to the diamonds. He waved to Calhoun. "Hi, Pop, remember me?"

Calhoun squinted his eyes and after a few seconds, nodded his head. "Where's Donnie Boy? Where's my grandson?"

"Rusty's coming Pop. He just got held up by the snow, I guess. I came to get my car." Calhoun made a face and tilted his head like the spotted dog in the Victrola ads. "I came for the car," McNairy repeated it, louder this time. "I came to get my car."

"These two come sneaking around," Calhoun said, gesturing with the rifle." Staying on track wasn't his long suit.

"You did good, Pop." McNairy nodded approval.

"I'm glad to see you, Mars," Jeffers said. "You have some things that belong to me. But first, take out your gun. Slow and easy." Vanner and LaSorda pulled their pieces and aimed them at me. I reached into my jacket, and pulled out my pistol. I held it out, handle first, by the barrel.

Jeffers said, with smug confidence, "Go get it."

Vanner shuffled through the snow and took the gun. He grinned, and with a vicious swipe, backhanded me across the forehead with it. I saw stars and nearly went over. I felt blood trickle down my face and wondered why it didn't freeze. Vanner shoved my pistol into the waistband of his pants and leered, "Not so smart now, are you, Mars?"

"He was smart enough to get this far," Jeffers said. He wasn't wearing a hat, and the snow was turning his chestnut hair white, making him look a lot older than his years. His eyes, behind steel rimmed glasses looked as cold as the snow. "But not as smart as he thinks he is." He stood eye to eye with me. "Now, give me the key— and the watch."

I nodded. "Okay. The watch is in my coat pocket." I started to reach for it when Jeffers grabbed a handful of Marge's hair and yanked her head back. He put a small automatic against her cheek. "No tricks, or your girlfriend here won't look quite the same."

"So what," Marge said. "You're going to kill us anyway, right?"

Jeffers smiled a thin smile that showed a little of his upper teeth. "True, but there's quick dead, and there's slow dead, that is, after the boys are done having their fun with you." He turned to me. "Now, the watch and the key."

I pulled the watch out of my coat pocket and held it by the chain. It swung like a gold pendulum. Jeffers let go of Marge's hair and took the watch without looking at it. "The key."

I reached into another pocket and pulled out one of the fakes. He took it and turned it in his fingers, studying it. "McNairy, is this it?"

Frank took the key and gave it the same close look Jeffers did. "Looks right."

"What do you mean, 'looks right?'"

"I haven't seen it for a couple of years."

Jeffers' eyes slid to the side. "I know you, Mars. You're no fool, but neither am I. You gave it up too easily; no resistance, no bravado, no bargaining. Now give me the real key."

I heaved a big sigh and shook my head. "You got me, Jeffers. Here's the real one." I pulled out the second fake. Jeffers nodded, satisfied at his own cleverness. "Now, Mister Calhoun, if you'd bring down your tractor, we'd like to pull the car out of the pond."

Pond? Marge and I looked at each other. I didn't see any pond.

"Right over there, Mars," McNairy said, pointing over my shoulder. I didn't see the pond from above because it had a thin scrim of ice over it, covered with snow.

Old man Calhoun headed for the tractor shed. "Okay, you're going to kill me anyway, Jeffers, and I know the diamonds are in the trunk. So, tell me, why did you kill Art McCurdy?"

"Tell him, McNairy."

"When I bought the Hudson, I had it delivered to McCurdy's garage. He was in the baby business before, and he knew the score: cooperate or else. Anything from framing him for car theft, which would put him in the jug this time, to putting the hurt on his family.

"McCurdy was as good as they come at his job, so I had him do some work on the Terraplane. He welded steel plate into the trunk and turned it into a rolling safe. You couldn't tell the difference from the outside, and you couldn't get into it with a stick of dynamite Unless . . ." he grinned. "You had the key."

"And now you do."

"McCurdy gave you up too, before he died. He said he painted a car for you."

"By the way, LaSorda," I snickered. "If you want your Packard back, it's parked at the Mount Summit Inn. I hope you like the new color."

LaSorda glared at me and Jeffers went on. "McCurdy was a loose end. Now he isn't." I thought about the implications of that statement, and decided that Marge and I were in the same category with Art.

Up the hill, the tractor rolled out of the shed, coughing and backfiring like an orange dragon. Black smoke belched out of its exhaust, and the tin can over the vertical pipe to keep out the rain rattled like a cowbell. Heavy tow chains clanked behind it. No wonder Calhoun was deaf as a post.

He drove the tractor past us and down to the edge of what I now recognized as the flat surface of an oval pond, about half as wide as it was long.

Jeffers said, "If you were wondering why you aren't dead yet, Mars, it's because none of us feels like taking a swim. The car's about ten feet in. Go hook the chains to the bumper."

The first step I took onto the ice, my foot went through up to my shin. The cold was painful. If I'd fallen through full body, I would probably have gone into shock, and for all I knew, my heart would have stopped. I swung the chain and broke a path for myself through the ice. By the time I was mid-thigh in the water, I was shivering. I wondered if Marge could hear my teeth chattering up on the bank.

A few more feet in, and I could feel a sharp drop off. I put a toe forward, and I felt something solid, the bumper of the Hudson. To loop the chain around the bumper and secure it, I'd have to crouch and go in the water chest deep.

I gritted my teeth and took the plunge. My hands found the bumper, but they were shaking so badly I fumbled with the chain and it took me a lot longer than I wanted it to. I straightened up, and I managed to hook the links together with a clevis. I climbed back onto the bank, my whole body shaking. Marge was looking at me, and I gave her a grin of confidence that I didn't really feel. At the moment, I didn't feel my feet either, and the rest of me was catching up.

Calhoun revved the tractor and the chain went taut. There was a tug of war between Allis Chalmers and gravity, but finally, the cleated tires of the tractor dug into the hill side, and it began crawling away from the pond.

The car's bumper emerged from the icy water first, then the hump of the trunk, the back window, the roof, and finally, the entire Hudson was on solid ground.

Jeffers started for the trunk, key in hand.

"Wait." McNairy held up a hand. "Hey, Pop, why don't you take these two," he jerked a thumb at Marge and me, "up to the house and wait for Rusty."

Sometimes, intuition comes in handy. I had a hunch and I played it. "Why don't you want him hanging around, Frank? Because you don't want him to see what's in the trunk?" I was shivering so hard I had to fight to get the words out. I turned to Calhoun and shouted so that he'd hear me, "Your Donnie Boy's dead, Calhoun. He's in the trunk. McNairy killed him." The words sunk in. I could see confusion on the old man's face, quickly turning to rage.

Frank grabbed the pistol from Vanner's hand.

"McNairy murdered Donnie Boy to keep all the loot for himself," I shouted. "He—"

Frank shot me. It felt like I was hit in the chest with a sledge hammer, but I was too numb from the cold to feel any pain. I went over backward in the snow. Marge screamed and started for me, but LaSorda put an arm around her neck.

I turned my head enough to see Calhoun raise his rifle and point it at Frank. "Is that true? Did you kill my Donnie Boy? Is that why he ain't come back all these years?"

"Put down the gun, you crazy old coot," LaSorda was pointing his automatic at Calhoun while he held Marge in front of him as a shield.

"Hell I will. Open that trunk, McNairy or I'll shoot you right where you stand."

Jeffers held out his hands, palms up, finger off the trigger of his pistol. "All right, Mister Calhoun," he shouted. "We'll open the trunk. I'm sure that what that man," he pointed to me, "told you is not true." He glared at McNairy, I guess he didn't like surprises either. He handed him the key. "Open it."

"I-"

Jeffers' hand closed on his pistol, and he aimed it at McNairy's head. Never taking his eyes off the old man, he hissed out of the corner of his mouth, "Open it. Now." He smiled reassuringly. "Mister Calhoun, if your grandson is in that trunk, I'll kill McNairy myself." Then to Frank, "Open it." Everybody had eyes on Frank as he put the key in the lock, everybody except Marge. She was looking at me when I opened one eye and winked.

Frank tried to turn the key, and it didn't budge.

"What's the matter?" Jeffers snarled. "Open it."

"Maybe it's stuck, "Frank said. "It's been underwater for years." He pulled they key out and ran his thumb over the ridges. He put it in the lock again and he still couldn't get it to turn.

McNairy and Jeffers both turned their heads at the same time to look at me. "It's another fake key. Mars still has the real one," Jeffers said. "Vanner, turn his pockets inside out. Find the damned thing."

Vanner crouched over me and started rifling my pockets. It took every bit of effort I could muster to play dead, which included not shivering, although I felt as if I'd eaten a snowman. He leaned across me to reach into my jacket, and I whispered in his ear, "You're not wearing your vest, I am."

I pulled my revolver out of his waistband and gave him two in the gut. He screamed and fell on top of me, pinning my gun hand. Everybody froze for a second, no pun intended, and then all hell broke loose. Calhoun fired his rifle and Frank's head burst open like a rotten tomato. Vanner and Jeffers both shot at once, and it was a tossup which of them killed Calhoun.

Jeffers' eyes were wild, his composure gone. He started in my direction gripping his automatic in both hands, aiming at my head, which was sticking out from under Vanner's shoulder. I couldn't move; Vanner lay on me groaning. Gut-shot is a bad, bad way to die.

"You've been a thorn in my foot this whole caper, Mars, but you've screwed things up for me for the last time." Jeffers cocked the hammer. "Give me the key."

"Eat shit." I pulled the trigger and the bullet went through Vanner, out his back, and into what I hoped was Jeffers' heart.

LaSorda threw Marge aside and drew a bead on me. I figured it was over, then I heard the blast of a shotgun, and LaSorda pitched forward and fell face down in the snow. Henry was standing up the hill, holding the other riot gun to his shoulder like he was posing for a statue of Daniel Boone.

My ears rang from the gunfire, but I could hear Henry say, "Just like Gangbusters."

Marge rolled Vanner's corpse off me. She pulled me into a sitting position and unzipped my jacket. McNairy's slug was lodged in the bullet-proof vest I took out of Vanner's car. It did enough damage, though. I coughed into my hand and brought it away bloody.

"I didn't mean to disobey your orders, Lieutenant," Henry apologized.

"But I saw that car pull in and I could see it wasn't anybody from around here. Figured it was the Dillinger mob and you might need some help."

"You did fine, Henry. Just like Gangbusters."

"Here comes the Cavalry." Marge pointed across the dale to the lane. The plow truck was in the lead, followed by two State Police cars with their spinners going.

"How did they know to come here?"

"I left a note on the front door of the hotel. I figured if Mason made it that far, he could go the rest of the distance. Looks like he brought some friends."

Mason brought a lot friends, as a matter of fact, including Czap and Montrose, the County Sheriff, and a half dozen State Troopers in their campaign hats. They got me on my feet and wanted to walk me to Calhoun's cabin, but I wouldn't let them.

"I have to know." I pulled the third key out of my pocket. "Let's open the trunk."

I offered the key to Czap, but he said, "You do the honors, Mars. You earned the right."

Mason held me up on one side and Marge on the other. My hand shook so badly that Marge had to help me guide the key into the slot. Mason snickered, and Marge shot him a dirty look. "No snide remarks, Cutter."

I turned the key and felt the lock move. Mason raised the lid, which was no easy feat, since it was plated with two-inch steel in stair-step layers, just like a safe. Two things were in the trunk besides the spare tire and the jack: a leather courier bag and a decomposed body with enough red hair left to I.D. it as Rusty Calhoun's.

I reached in and pulled out the bag. Its lock had been sprung, and when I put my hand inside, I pulled out two cloth pouches. I poured one into my palm and diamonds spilled out. Ice on ice.

"Congratulations, Mars," Czap said, "You've cracked the case."

"Now," said Marge, "let's get him out of those wet clothes so he can live to celebrate it."

They carried me up to Calhoun's house and wrapped me in blankets that smelled so foul, I'd've almost rather frozen. Marge helped me out of the wet jacket, shirt and vest. In the middle of my chest, a bruise the size of my open hand was darkening. It'd be a week or two before I could do pushups without screaming.

I sat in a rocking chair thawing out beside the Franklin stove. Mason handed me a flask and I took a good pull on it. After Henry's moonshine, Seagram's Seven went down like club soda.

Czap pulled up a chair in front of me. "Okay, Mars, tell me all about it."

"Chrissakes, George," Mason complained, " give him a break. He's been beaten, shot, and frozen."

I held up a hand. "No problem, guys. I'll tell you the whole story as soon as I . . ." My head sunk onto my chest, and I wasn't faking. I didn't wake up 'til the next afternoon. When I did, I was in a hospital bed. I saw a pitcher of water and flowers on the stand beside me. Why do they always send flowers? Maybe they're trying to beat the rush for the funeral.

I raised my head and looked around the room. The other bed was empty. Mason and Marge were sitting in chairs near the door. Marge noticed I was awake and elbowed Mason. "He's conscious."

"Too bad," Mason said, faking annoyance. "I was hoping I'd have the office all to myself."

"Glad to see you too, Mason." I raised my hands. "No cuffs. I guess Czap didn't arrest me."

"Pending further investigation.' But we all know that by the time this shakes out, you'll be in the clear."

I lowered my voice. "What about Legatto?"

Mason laughed. "You don't have to whisper, Ike. There're no cops outside. Robbery, pure and simple. He got off a shot, the other guy got off a shot. They aren't looking too hard for the shooter. Off the record, Agronski's feelings are 'good riddance.'"

"What about Kobie and Watts?"

Seems the slugs they pulled out of your vest and Calhoun's head matched the ones they dug out of the Bobbsey Twins. You obviously didn't shoot yourself. You're clear on that one."

"The car?"

"Turns out it was hot anyway," Mason said. "LaSorda got it from some wheel thief in Republic. The owner's in Morgantown, West Virginia. Of course, there's that little matter of you impersonating a police officer, but prosecuting you would be like prosecuting George Washington, the way the press is painting you. I'm guessing that charge will go away, too."

"So, all's right with the world, huh?"

Marge broke in. "There's still a little matter of that cruise."

Mason stood up. "I'll leave that discussion to the two of you."

XXIV

The next day, Marge brought me the newspapers with the story about cracking the diamond heist. Along with the papers, Marge had a box from Dobbs under her arm. It was a new fedora.

"I just got a new hat a couple days ago," I said.

"Look in the band."

I take a nine. The band sized the hat at ten-and-a-half.

"That's to accommodate your swelled head after you read your ink."

The *Press* carried the same picture of me that they were ready to put numbers across the chest of a week before. The headline across the top of the *Post Gazette* read: Private Eye Finds Diamonds, Clears Self. The *Sun-Telegraph* carried the banner: Suspected Cop-Killer Proves Hero.

The papers got most of it right; of course, there were a few details missing, but those would go to my grave with me, or maybe send me to my grave early if I gave them up. The *Press* had the best version, but that was because they had an exclusive interview with Marge and Mason. I hoped they'd give her a raise as a reward, or maybe a vacation.

"Anything else you need, Mars?"

"I could use a pint of gin, but I don't think it's allowed in here."

"Maybe I can sneak it in under my garter and pour it in your I.V."

I laughed, and it hurt. "I'm about out of cigarettes. And yeah, there is one thing I do want."

"What's that?"

"A radio. I want to tune in to *Gangbusters*."

That afternoon, I was dozing when Czap and Montrose came in to see me. Maybe they thought that if they woke me up, I'd be too groggy to sell them a song and dance. I knew it was coming, though, and I was ready to lie and swear to it. So were Marge and Mason. We had worked out what seemed a plausible enough story, given a little tolerance for stretching.

"Start talking, Mars." He lit a cigarette and didn't offer me one. No need to play Mister Nice Guy today; we both knew the score. Jeffers was crooked, Kobylarz and Watts were crooked; hell, most of the City was crooked. There was no shortage of targets for finger pointing.

"You, know as well as I do, George, everybody in Pittsburgh's up to something shady, except you and me."

"And sometimes I don't have to wonder about you, Mars. I know there's more to this than you're telling me."

"What don't you know? Everybody wanted the diamonds. McNairy engineered a successful heist in spite of bad luck and fate. Jeffers swiped the key to the Hudson from evidence, but only McNairy knew where the car was hidden. He killed Donovan Calhoun before they ever got to the farm, locked him in the trunk with the loot, and rolled the car into the pond. The old man was loony as Daffy Duck and the perfect patsy. Anybody came near the place, he'd shoot them for Revenuers.

"Jimmy Cramer burgled Jeffers' house and stole the key. He was going to sell it back to Jeffers, who was using Kobylarz and Watts as his errand boys. Somehow, McNairy's accomplices, Patsy Donohoe and Marty Gallagher, got wind of it, and they ambushed Cramer. I happened along at an opportune moment, and Jimmy gave me the key. That wound the clock."

"Hold on. I can see this so far, but why did Cramer give you the key?"

"He was dying. Maybe he just didn't want Gallagher and Donohoe to have it, kind of a spit-in-the -eye gesture. You know." I put my index finger at the corner of my eye and pulled down the lid.

"The crooked cops show up, and before they have a chance to search Cramer or me for the key, you show up, and I walk with the key in my pocket. The Bobbsey Twins find out Cramer doesn't have the key, and they roust me for it. That goes south, and I leave them knocked out in the grocery store. They wake up and call Jeffers, who sends LaSorda and Vanner to take care of the loose ends and frame me for it.

"Jeffers doesn't know for sure if I have the key, but to cover all his bases, he has the whole police force doing his dirty work for him, looking for me on the phony homicide rap. I go on the run, and have to figure out the whole business before somebody puts a hole through me. It's simple, right?"

"Almost." Czap flicked the ash off his cigarette onto the floor. "Jeffers had a picture in his pocket of that homemade key and a pocket watch. He had that watch on him when we took him to the morgue."

Montrose weighed in. "We found these in that beat-up suitcase of yours at the Summit Inn. He pulled out the strip with the other three snaps from the photo booth, still attached in a chain. "The picture in Jeffers' pocket matches these three to a T."

He held them in front of my face. "Look close, Mars. See the watch showing out of the cuff in the last picture?" He reached in his pocket and pulled out my waterlogged Bulova, stopped at eleven-twenty-two. "Look familiar?"

I shrugged, which made me wince because my chest still hurt like hell. "If you put out an APB for a man toting a Bulova oyster, you'll only pull in maybe ten thousand suspects."

Czap nodded. "I'm gonna let that one slide, Mars, because you took a bunch of rotten potatoes out of the bin."

"Trouble is, George, there are only about a thousand more waiting to take their places. Like I said about you and me."

"You're getting away with something, Mars. I'm just not sure exactly what it is—yet."

"Don't stay up nights worrying about it, George. It gives you wrinkles."

They left, and I breathed a sigh of relief—for now.

Later that afternoon, three men in suits came into the room. One of them handed me a card introducing him as Marvin Katz of the Pittsburgh Diamond Exchange. Another's card ID'd him as William Reynolds from the Hartford Fire Insurance Company. I never did find out who the third guy was. He must have been out of cards.

"We are very grateful to you, Mister Mars," Katz said. "Your return of the diamonds to us has settled a number of difficult issues." He shot a look at Reynolds. No love lost there. Probably why neither introduced the other. My experience with insurance companies is that everything's fine as long as you're paying them money, but if they have to pay you ten cents, it has to be pried out of their fingers with a crowbar.

Reynolds ignored him. "Mister Mars," he said, "as a gesture of the Hartford Fire Insurance Company's gratitude, I would like to present you with this check and say thank you."

Okay, I thought, you'd like to. Are you going to really do it?

He did. "Thank you, Mister Mars." he handed me a cashier's check from the Iron and Glass Bank for five hundred dollars. A drop in the bucket compared to the hundred grand they paid to settle the claim and would now get back from the Diamond Exchange.

"As Mister Reynolds said, Mister Mars, we are all very grateful for your help. If there is anything that I or the Exchange can do for you, please don't hesitate to ask."

I nodded. "Let me think about it."

XXV

The next morning, I quit coughing up blood, and the doctors said I could go home in one more day. Marge brought in a radio, and we spent a quiet afternoon holding hands and listening to Benny Goodman, Artie Shaw, and Paul Whiteman. She didn't bring me the gin, but I really didn't need it. The dope they shot me up with every four hours kept me in and out of a doze all day.

"Guess what I bought today?" Marge said, one of those times when I was awake.

"A race horse?" I had a pretty good idea what the right answer was, but I couldn't resist playing it for all I could. "Rights to a gold mine in Colorado?"

"Even better than that."She held up an envelope with tickets showing. "Cunard passage for two on the Queen Mary, round trip to London."

"Where'd you get that kind of money?"

"Found it in your pants pocket."

That's my Marge.

She was smart enough to book the cruise for two weeks later to give me time to recuperate. When I got back to my apartment, I found that Marge had cleaned the place up, filled the refrigerator, and put a carton of Lucky Strikes and a fifth of Old Grand Dad in the kitchen cupboard. She came home every day from work and cooked me supper, and treated me like a king. I almost hated to get well.

When we got on the Queen Mary, Mason came to see us off. He showed me the front page of the *Pittsburgh Tattler*, a local scandal sheet. There was Gloria Swenson's photo beside one of her husband Willis. The headline read: Stockbroker Dumps Cheating Wife. Jilted Chauffeur Blows Whistle."There goes a paying client," Mason said.

"Not to worry, Mason. There'll be two more like her next week. Human nature keeps us in groceries."

XXVI

The Queen Mary was a floating version of the William Penn, with twice the personal service. I couldn't sneeze without one of the white-jacketed attendants appearing magically at my elbow with a handkerchief. I didn't light my own cigarette once the whole way to London. The staterooms were almost as big as hotel rooms, too. Marge spared no expense with Gus's money. Hey, I figure, easy come, easy go. Besides, she deserved it for sticking by me all the way.

We'd have dinner in the dining room every night, and dance in the ballroom to a full orchestra. When Marge told me I had to buy a tuxedo for the trip, I thought she was kidding, but I wore it every night of the voyage.

In the day time, we'd sit under lap robes on the observation deck in those comfy canvas lounge chairs you can't buy anywhere, drinking hot tea laced with honey and rum and watching for icebergs and whales across the endless green waves. Marge and I avoided the subject of the Diamond Caper all this time. That's what vacations are for; vacate the premises, and all the crap that goes with them.

One afternoon, she finally brought it up. "Mars, aren't you worried that the Mob or somebody's going to come after you for revenge? You took out a lot of their people."

"I've thought about that," I said. "I think the Mob is glad to be rid of McNairy. Somebody who's always trying to prove something is a liability. Jeffers stepped off the path. He figured to grab the diamonds all for himself, probably kill McNairy in the bargain. Maybe McNairy planned to kill Jeffers and his crew, then stiff his partners. Jeffers was doing all this behind the Organization's back without giving them their cut. It's a wash where the Mob is concerned, so they have no quarrel with me."

She let that sink in for a while and finally said, "I feel like we're in a movie, like *The Thin Man*."

"I like that idea. Maybe I could trade in my badge and gun for Hollywood. I'm sure they'd be happy to hire me."

"You don't have the looks—" Marge in mid sentence when she saw my face, the image of William Powell. "You can change again. When did that happen?"

"A week or so after I lost the gift, it came back." I covered my face with my newspaper as a couple strolled past arm in arm. "Now if you could just look like Myrna Loy, we could tell MGM we'll work for half what they're paying Powell."

"What you see is what you get, Mars."

I let my face slip back to my old self. "And it's plenty good enough for me." I kissed her for a minute, and we both settled back in our chairs.

"You know, Mars, I could get used to this kind of living. It's too bad we didn't find those diamonds and lam before the bad guys and the good guys all showed up."

"Yeah, you're right. Speaking of diamonds." I reached under my lap robe and pulled out a small box covered in red velvet. "Katz said if there was anything he could do for me, just ask, so I did." I flipped open the box and Marge's eyes got wide when she saw the diamond set in a filigreed gold band. "Coincidentally, it's one of the rocks from McNairy's trunk. I thought that would make it even more special."

Her eyes teared up. "Well, are you going to ask me, Mars?"

"Do I have to?"

"On bended knee, Buster"

About Our Creators

Writer-

FRED ADAMS, JR. is a retired Penn State University English Professor who spends his days writing pulp fiction and his nights working as a singer-songwriter. His Sam Dunne novel *Dead Man's Melody* was nominated as Pulp Novel of the Year in 2017's Pulp Factory Awards, and his Smith Brothers novel *The Eye of Quang-Chi* was nominated for the same award in 2018. His titles include *Hitwolf* 1 and 2, *Six Gun Terrors* vols. 1, 2, and 3, and *C.O. Jones: Mobsters and Monsters, Skinners*, and *The Damned and the Doomed*. His original Sherlock Holmes anthology *The Affair of the Chronic Argonaut* was recently published by Pro Se Press. Forthcoming titles from Airship 27 include *C.O. Jones: Home Front, Six Gun Terrors 4: The Town Killers*, a Sam Dunne Mystery, *Blood is the New Black*, and *Holster Full of Death*, a Dead Sheriff novel. He lives in Mount Pleasant, Pennsylvania in "perpetual terror of boredom."

Visit Fred's website at http://drphreddee.com/author

Illustrator-

JAMES MCFARLAND - is a commercial illustrator, fine artist, and graphic designer with over a decade of experience. Goal-oriented project management is not only his methodology; it is his manner of life. He studied Fine Arts and Graphic Design, later Mechanical Engineering and Drafting. He has made his home in lots of places over the years, including Denver, Seattle, Portland, Spokane, Alaska, Poulsbo, and many rural towns.

www.jjamesdesignandillustration.com

BOOKS BY FRED ADAMS JR.

FRED ADAMS JR. PULP WRITER

SIX-GUN TERRORS
SIX-GUN TERRORS Vol One
SIX-GUN TERRORS   Vol Two
SIX-GUN TERRORS Vol Three — The Slithering Terror

HITWOLF
HITWOLF
HITWOLF 2 — The Pack

C.O. JONES
C.O. JONES
C.O. JONES — Skinners
C.O. JONES — The Damned and the Doomed

SAM DUNNE MYSTERIES
Dead Man's Melody

THE SMITH BROTHERS SERIES
The Eye of Quang Chi

IKE MARS MYSTERIES
The Bloody Key